Ben was putting his life on the line... for her.

The headlights grew brighter from behind.

"Hold on." Ben accelerated and passed the 18-wheeler.

Was it too much to hope for that they could lose their followers?

Chasey was starting to think she could have done better on her own instead of going into WITSEC, because then she would always be on the lookout and keep a low profile, rather than relaxing into a new identity. Trusting in hope for a normal life that was beginning to look further and further out of her reach.

The speedy Suburban gained on them.

"Bennnnn?"

"I see it. Hold on and pray."

Terror consumed her, invading all the spaces of her heart. Chasey closed her eyes and tried. She could only think to call out to God.

She felt the sudden jolt as the Suburban bumped the sedan, sending it fishtailing until it became a full-on spin across the road. Terror in her heart spilled over and flooded her body. The sedan left the road, bouncing and cascading into a snow-filled ditch...

Elizabeth Goddard is the award-winning author of more than thirty novels and novellas. A 2011 Carol Award winner, she was a double finalist in the 2016 Daphne du Maurier Award for Excellence in Mystery/Suspense, and a 2016 Carol Award finalist. Elizabeth graduated with a computer science degree and worked in high-level software sales before retiring to write full-time.

Books by Elizabeth Goddard

Love Inspired Suspense

Mount Shasta Secrets

Deadly Evidence
Covert Cover-Up
Taken in the Night
High Stakes Escape

Coldwater Bay Intrigue

Thread of Revenge
Stormy Haven
Distress Signal
Running Target

Wilderness, Inc.

Targeted for Murder
Undercover Protector
False Security
Wilderness Reunion

Visit the Author Profile page at Harlequin.com for more titles.

High Stakes Escape

Elizabeth Goddard

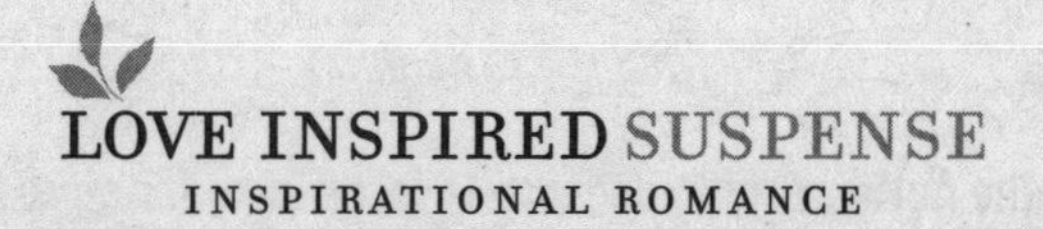

LOVE INSPIRED® SUSPENSE
INSPIRATIONAL ROMANCE

ISBN-13: 978-1-335-72266-9

High Stakes Escape

This edition published by arrangement with Harlequin Books S.A.

For questions and comments about the quality of this book, please contact us at CustomerService@Harlequin.com.

Love Inspired
22 Adelaide St. West, 40th Floor
Toronto, Ontario M5H 4E3, Canada
www.Harlequin.com

Printed in U.S.A.

I will lift up mine eyes unto the hills,
from whence cometh my help. My help cometh
from the Lord, which made heaven and earth.

—*Psalm* 121:1–2

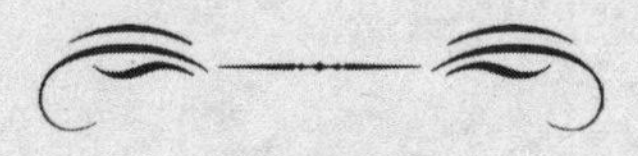

To Andrew, my fierce warrior.

ONE

Deputy US Marshal Ben Bradley stared at the covered body being retrieved by the medical examiner, struggling with disbelief. How could this brutal murder have happened here in this comfortable home situated in the quiet middle-class neighborhood in Snohomish, Washington, near Seattle? Minivans were parked in driveways. Kids played safely in their yards or in the park across the street even as fall temperatures quickly shifted colder. This place was supposed to be safe. The resident who had lived there was supposed to be hidden. Anonymous. Protected.

But inside this sheltered haven, a vicious crime had been committed.

Disturbing.

He stood outside the crime scene tape with the neighbors who looked on, and he listened to their murmurs, their shock joining his own disbelief. He didn't have to look at their faces to know he would see a mixture of horror and grief. Tears and suspicions.

Fear.

At the moment, no children played at the park across the street. They had all been gathered into their homes until it was safe. He could hear the people's unspoken questions—will the neighborhood ever be the same? Will it ever be safe again?

Unfortunately, he had no way to soothe their fears, no way to tell them that the killer would not return.

After all, the killer had already taken out the only person in witness protection in this neighborhood.

Ben drew in a few calming breaths to slow his pounding heart, and pushed back the confusion and rage that prevented him from moving.

Now it was time to get to work.

Ducking under the yellow tape that established the crime scene perimeter, he approached the officer holding a clipboard. Ben flashed his credentials. The officer arched a brow and handed over the board. Ben signed his name on the scene security log and dutifully stuck to the "path of contamination" as it was called, established to protect evidence and keep the crime scene locked down. He didn't bother donning plastic booties or gloves like the evidence techs. After all, he had no reason to get close to the body. He wasn't there to investigate, just to verify…and inform. Inside the house, Ben headed for the man in a Giants ball cap who was writing in a notebook. He assumed this man was the detective, but the cap made him look a little out of place in this scenario.

Ben once again held up his credentials. "Inspector Ben Bradley, US Marshals Service."

The man continued to write in the notebook then finally eyed Ben. "I'm Detective Wright. What can I do for you?"

"What can you tell me about what's happened here?"

Wright took his time studying Ben, as if considering how much to share. "You being here… She's one of yours then." A statement rather than a question.

Ben's demeanor sobered even more as he nodded. His very presence seemed to answer all their questions about why she'd been murdered. Anyone in law enforcement knew the US Marshals Service handled the witness protection program.

"Well, that tells me something." Wright shut his notebook. "Looks like a forced entry, and the rest you can see for yourself."

Ben glanced around the chaotic scene. Overturned lamps, coffee table and chairs. His heart ached at the thought of her struggle to live. He hated the images that fought for space in his mind, but he couldn't shut off the way the brutal crime seemed to play across his vision as if it were happening right now. Sheila Redgrave, formerly Shelly Rodman, had fought to the very end. She'd thrown the lamp. Turned over the coffee table as she'd fought to survive. She'd obviously tried to escape through the sliding-glass door that opened into the backyard, but she hadn't made it. The bloodstained carpet near the door told of her demise.

Grief twisted his insides. Beyond that, he struggled to wrap his mind around it—how could this have happened in this new life where she was supposed to be safe? *Oh... Shelly. What did you do? Who did you talk to?*

Had Shelly been complicit in her own demise and unintentionally given away her true identity? Or could her death have been a failure on his part? The murder of someone to whom he'd given a new identity and placed in the WITSEC—Witness Security—program weighed on him like nothing else.

"Cause of death?" Ben hadn't looked at the covered body the medical examiner had wheeled away on a gurney. Maybe he should have, but he hadn't been able to bring himself to look. Heaviness settled in his gut, and he could barely hold it together.

"The ME will have the final say, of course," Wright said, "but she suffered two knife wounds, which I suspect were fatal."

Once again, Ben studied the bloodstained carpet.

"We'll conduct an investigation. Talk to neighbors and fa—"

Ben held up his hand and stopped the man midsentence. "This is where I step in. Talk to the neighbors and this community who knew Sheila Redgrave, but she doesn't exist beyond that. Don't go looking for any family. Do you understand?"

Wright held his notebook under his arm and fisted his hands on his hips. "So you're certain this has to do with her past."

Ben shrugged. "I could be wrong. Let me know if you have any local leads."

He wouldn't say more. But given that three days ago he'd had to move WITSEC's Susan Lively from his residence of three years in St. Louis, Missouri—giving her an entirely new identity and new home in Salt Lake City—because Susan had been attacked in her home, Ben's internal warning system was going off. He was in charge of handling a number of witnesses at any one time, delivering them to trial and then to their new lives. And sometimes, relocating and arranging new identities for those whose original new identities had been compromised.

That rarely happened, and now suddenly two of his witnesses had been discovered.

The detective took in the scene around him again. "Mind letting me know if you discover it's related to her past? That way we can close the case."

"Of course. And, Detective, not a word of this. I'll speak to your superior, as well." Ben took a step away. "Mind if I look around?"

"Keep to the path if you're not going to put on the gloves and booties. We might be small-town but we know how to investigate."

"Of course." Ben nodded and walked the hallway until he found what he assumed was Sheila's bedroom. He'd set her up to work as a customer service representative for a credit card company far away from her previous job as a financial assistant to a Wall Street mogul. That way she could continue using her skills but in a safe place.

He found a photograph of Sheila with a guy, his arm wrapped around her shoulders. There was a waterfall behind them. She looked happy and maybe even in love. His heart sank even more. She'd been successfully making a new life and now…this. Ben would let the detective inform the boyfriend. Ben would be the one to tell her aunt and uncle who'd raised her. She'd only spoken to them once since she'd left her old life behind, and that via the marshals' offices.

They would want to know why, and would probably think that the system had failed their niece. They would not be the only ones who wanted answers. Ben wanted to know why she'd been attacked in her home and murdered. And…he thought the same thing they would think—that *he'd* failed their niece.

He stepped outside the house and US Deputy Marshal Silas Tate approached, his lips forming a deep frown. "I got here as soon as I could."

He trusted his fellow deputy Silas.

Ben had asked for help from the Eastern District of California because something was messed up. Though Ben worked out of this district, he could place witnesses anywhere in the country—whatever was required to keep them safe.

"I know." Unfortunately, not fast enough.

"Do you think this was a hit or something local?"

Ben wasn't ready to voice his thoughts yet, especially with an audience—including some reporters he saw milling around. He headed for his vehicle and got in.

Silas joined him so they could speak privately, then leaned in. "Given that Susan was attacked three days ago and now Redgrave… I gotta say I'm a little concerned."

"You and me both." Ben got on his cell and called his supervisor, Assistant Chief Deputy James Calvin, to request that all the witnesses he'd placed be moved immediately. Maybe he was overreacting, but he didn't want to risk lives. Better to take precautions.

Ben's thoughts kept going to one witness in particular—Chasey. Panic rose in his chest. Was he already too late?

The black sedan with dark windows drew her attention as it slowly made its way down the road.

A little too slowly, if anyone asked her. Chasey Cook's anxiety inched up.

She shook it off as best she could. She was just being paranoid. No one could find her. She continued her jog along the paved trails that wound through the woods in the small park. She took in the grass to her left and pine needles to her right. Across the way and through the trees, she spotted a playground. But at this time of day, kids were just getting out of school.

Maybe having an afternoon snack before they took to the playground. There was no one around…no one to see her if she got grabbed.

Stop that! she scolded. She wasn't going to get grabbed. She was fine. Safe.

Her breaths were steady and even as she breathed in the scent of evergreens and fresh mountain air. Running in small-town northern California with Mt. Shasta visible in the distance was such a different experience than she'd had before, living the big-city life that used to be hers. Until a year ago…

In her peripheral vision, she spotted the black vehicle again—through the trees and far from her.

The sedan has nothing to do me. It's nothing. I don't need to worry about anything but enjoying this beautiful day.

If her boss, the dean of the English department at the small community college, hadn't given his office Friday afternoon off, she wouldn't have been able to take advantage of daylight in the park. The days were already growing shorter well into autumn. As if to confirm her thoughts, a cold breeze with the hint of an arctic bite wrapped around her. Actually, it felt nice considering she'd worked up a sweat under her light jacket.

The paved trail weaved around the spruce

and cedar trees, and Chasey kept waiting for that moment when the tension would drain out of her. A cold rain droplet landed on her face. Her signal to head home. She jogged across the street to the neighborhood where her cozy bungalow was located, only about three blocks down.

No matter how she tried to ignore the sudden paranoia, a shudder crawled over her that she just couldn't let go.

Paranoid or not, she flipped around to jog backward, checking behind her just in case.

There was that black sedan again.

Why, why, why...

Heart pounding, Chasey ran faster and cut across two yards to head to her house. But she stopped behind the neighbor's house. She pressed her hands against her thighs and caught her breath. Calmed her nerves.

No...her nerves were not going to calm.

At her neighbor Jill Samson's house, Chasey moved to the back corner closest to her own property and crouched behind a bush. She remained in the shadows and inched forward enough so that she could peer at the house she'd turned into a home and had grown to love in the last year. She never could have believed she could so quickly embrace a new life, a new identity and find new friends. People to love and care about. And yet, God had given her that.

Was today the day she would lose it all?

Heart pounding, she squeezed her eyes shut. *What should I do, Lord? Direct me, guide my path.*

The little bungalow she'd decorated herself. That house she'd made into…well, a home, could already be compromised.

She couldn't let that happen.

And yet, if she went inside, she could be walking into a death trap.

A cold mist filled the air and dusk would be on her soon. If she left now, she would literally be fleeing into the night. She drew in a deep, cold breath.

It was now or never.

She had to face whatever waited for her before Jill or other neighbors inserted themselves into her life and got hurt. Because of her.

She took one step out from behind Jill's house and waited. Nothing. No gunfire. So she continued forward. Chasey crept over to the back door and unlocked it. Stepping inside, she waited again for a few moments, listening. Silence met her ears.

The scent of her favorite vanilla-honey air freshener filled her nose. The house felt peaceful and still. For the moment, she breathed easier. But she wouldn't allow herself to be fooled by appearances. Not when her instincts were still screaming that danger was closing in.

Racing through the house, she grabbed her purse and her tablet, grateful that she already had her cell on her. Those were the most essential items. Plus a warmer jacket.

One last look around the place she'd called home…all her thrift shop collections. If the worst had happened and she'd been found, she would probably never be back here again.

Chasey cracked the garage door off the kitchen open.

Pain ignited in her head.

Someone yanked her back into the house by her hair. Screaming, she fell against the kitchen counter as he released her hair. Gasping for breath, she felt the fear ignite her drive to live. A man lunged for her and she ducked away, barely avoiding his grip, then scrambled to the other side of the table, instinctively putting something between them. Sucking in air, she searched the room. What could she use as a weapon?

The lamp she'd found at a secondhand shop was the closest object. Chasey lunged for it and wrapped her fingers around the base. She lifted it and felt the object's weight, then threw it at his head. Of course, he dodged the lamp. The entertainment center was behind her. She reached around and grabbed a stack of DVDs, which she then tossed at him one by one with all the force she could muster, believing—hoping—they would deter him at least for a few seconds longer. But she was only fooling herself.

He continued forward and reached for her. Once again, she dodged his grip.

She had to make it out of here, but he stood between her and the front door. Between her and the garage door. Behind her, though, was an open path to the back door through which she'd entered the house. Could she dash through the door fast enough to make it out? If she did escape, she could run for help. Unless he was a runner, he wouldn't catch her. And maybe, if she could get to someplace crowded, with other people around as witnesses, he'd be more reluctant to chase after her.

Torn over where she should go, what she should do, the only thing she knew for certain was that she had to get away. Right. Now.

She made a mad dash for the back door even as he snagged the purse that hung over her shoulder and yanked.

She released her purse and he fell backward

away from her, giving her the chance to push through the back door. She bounded down the steps and landed in the yard.

Freedom.

She raced around the side of the house. If she could just get to her car before he stopped her… But as she reached the driveway, she saw that was no longer an option. His black sedan blocked her car's exit from the garage. She ran around to the driver's side of his car, wondering if she could hide in there, and unfortunately found the door locked.

That was okay. She had her cell in her jacket pocket. She could call for help. Running down the street, she found a space between two houses and called 9-1-1. Behind her, she heard tires squeal out of her driveway.

He was still after her. Still determined to find and kill her.

She'd have to keep moving. She continued jogging down the street as she told the 9-1-1 operator that someone was trying to kill her. No, she couldn't stay in one place and wait for the police. She had to lose him first. Dispatch said that the nearest officer was on his way.

That was great, but again, she couldn't stay in one place long enough to wait for them. Still, she would look for a police cruiser even as she tried to hide from her pursuer. She'd described the sedan and given the license plate number so that maybe the police could stop the man after her.

She cut through neighborhoods.

The marina…

Her pursuer was in a car. He wouldn't catch her in a boat. She jogged toward the marina as the air grew colder. Her nose had started running, too. All she needed now was for the sky to open up and let loose.

Except… Was it sleeting?

Great.

Whatever. Of course she would be running for her life as the weather decided to take a turn for the nasty.

All she had to do was to get across the lake, hopefully before dark so she'd have a chance to try to find some shelter.

She'd already lost him for now, but she wouldn't take any chances. She wanted to get completely out of his reach forever. The summer crowd had already removed their boats from the marina, but the fishing crowd loved the cooler temperatures for brown and rainbow trout.

Chasey untied then hopped into a small V-shaped fishing boat and started the motor. She'd find a way to return it, but right now, she needed to survive. She steered the boat out onto the lake. A couple of other boats were closer to shore, but looked like they were heading back in. Hardly surprising, given the approaching nightfall along with inclement weather.

Could her pursuer have picked a better time?

Chasey steered the boat straight across the small lake. She should get across in a few minutes, and then what, she wasn't sure, but somehow, she would make sure that he wouldn't find her.

The sound of a motor starting up echoed across the lake. She glanced behind her. Another boat angled out of the marina and was headed her direction.

What?

Oh no…

Heart pounding, she fished out her cell phone and tried the most important call she could make. The call of her life. She let the man who could save her know what was happening. When she finished the call, Chasey glanced at her cell and realized the battery was dead. Had any part of her call to him gone through or was she truly on her own?

Just get across the lake.

Find somewhere safe where you can wait.

Yet, even as she tried to concentrate on steering the boat, she couldn't help asking how this could have happened.

How could someone have found Kelly Cabot in her new life?

TWO

Ben pulled right up to the curb in front of the house that now belonged to Chasey Cook—formerly known as Kelly Cabot. He hopped out of the vehicle and didn't bother closing the car door as he ran up to the front entrance. He'd brought a contingency of deputy marshals with him, and they surrounded the house. WITSEC inspectors worked alone for the most part and, usually even within the field offices, their function was known only to a few to keep their witnesses' identities safe, even from law enforcement, who might be pressured or coerced. Ben wasn't used to ordering other marshals around. But these were extraordinary circumstances.

He pounded on the door. "Chasey! Miss Cook, it's Deputy Marshal Ben Bradley."

Silas Tate opened the door from the inside and let him in, surprising Ben.

"She's not here," Silas said. "The back door was open, so I entered the premises."

An opened back door was a bad sign. Ben stepped inside and the sight that met him twisted his insides into multiple knots. All of it…was a bad sign. He'd seen a similar scene at Sheila's home—just as much mess, just as much chaos indicating a struggle. His only comfort was that, so far, he didn't see bloodstained rugs or crimson spills on the wood floors. For that, he should be relieved. But Chasey had definitely been in a fight.

Heart pounding in his throat, he pressed his palms to his eyes. "We have to find her before it's too late." They all knew this, but Ben needed to express his frustration. He released the anger through the bite in his tone.

Ben glanced to the door at the exact moment a local police officer stepped through.

He aimed his gun at Ben and Silas, who stood behind him. "Police. Don't move."

"Deputy US Marshal Ben Bradley and Deputy US Marshal Silas Tate at your service, Officer. I'm going to reach for my credentials."

The officer nodded.

Ben slowly reached for his badge wallet inside his jacket pocket and pulled it out, holding his credentials so they were displayed. The officer approached and then put his weapon away. Ben noted the officer's badge number.

"I'm Officer Richard Pelman. Dispatch received an emergency call," he said. "Chasey Cook lives at this address. She said that she was being pursued and was in danger."

That news should come as no surprise, but hearing the words out loud from the officer was like a stranglehold around Ben's throat. He struggled to get enough air to speak.

Then finally he asked, "Have you found her?" Ben held on to hope.

"No. I've driven around the neighborhood but didn't see her. I didn't see the black sedan she mentioned, either. Instead I found you guys in her house."

"She's in trouble. We're here to help her," Ben said. "And we also need your help."

Officer Pelman studied Ben. "I'll do what I can. What would you like me to do? I could secure the crime scene here."

"In due time. Right now, we need to find Chasey. Please continue to patrol the neighborhood and look for her—or for anything out of the ordinary that might clue us in to where she's gone. We need to get to her before it's too late. Her life is in imminent danger."

Officer Pelman's expression was somber as he nodded and exited the house. Ben squeezed his fists, anxiety crawling over him. He thought to try her again on his cell phone, but instead he found a call from her. His cell had been on vibrate, but he hadn't felt it!

Good girl, Chasey. She should have called him long before now, but maybe she hadn't had a chance while someone was in serious pursuit and she was on the run. Ben listened to her garbled and broken-up message, her words breathless and panicked.

"Ben, it's me, Chasey… Um, Kelly… I think he found me—" a sob cracked, and she gasped "—I don't know if you'll get this message in time, but I need your help. I don't know… I don't know if I can outrun him. I'm at the marina—"

The call went dead.

His heart twisted with his already tangled-up gut.

"The lake. The marina. She's at the marina!" he shouted.

He raced to his vehicle while shouting instructions for the other marshals to help. Two deputies stayed behind at the house to protect her in case she returned and to watch for anyone who might come looking for her. Two others would walk the neighborhood on foot, looking for her. Silas hopped into the vehicle with him.

Lord, what is going on?

Susan. Sheila. And now Chasey.

If only he had acted sooner… But this attack on WITSEC witnesses, in particular those for whom Ben had secured new identities, had unfolded fast and Ben had simply been blindsided. Who was behind the brutality and why?

Questions bombarded him even as he focused on the only thing that was truly important in this one moment in time: saving Chasey. The woman Ben had fallen for when he'd been assigned to protect her for a few months before she'd testified at her uncle's trial.

Ben steered from the curb and resisted the urge to speed through the neighborhood. He wouldn't risk hurting innocent bystanders getting home from work or stopping to get their mail. Still, it felt surreal to see them and realize that life went on around him as though nothing nefarious was at play.

When he exited the neighborhood onto a two-lane road, his tires squealed as Ben floored it and headed toward the lake and the marina. At the water's edge, he drove past a few buildings. The pier was up ahead. He didn't bother to park the car but stopped in the middle of the asphalt parking lot. Hopping out of his vehicle, he jogged over to the few boats moored along the peer. The sky looked gray and heavy with precipitation that threatened to make the dark of night move in even sooner.

"Chasey!" he shouted.

Ben and Silas removed their weapons from their holsters. If she had an active pursuer, they might come across the man—or worse, find the man engaged in attacking Chasey. He could only hope she'd found a good place to hide and the man had not found her here yet.

God help me find her first and keep her safe!

He and Silas searched around the marina buildings, then opened up the warehouse to search inside. No one was there. Maybe they closed up shop early on Friday.

"Chasey! It's Ben. You can come out now. You're safe. Where are you?" His words echoed through the warehouse that was filled with boating supplies and parts but was otherwise empty—at least empty of life.

Nothing.

Come on, Chasey, where could you be? Ben called her phone and texted her again, but got no response. Was he too late? Please let him not be too late.

Where could she have gone? Maybe… Maybe she'd actually taken a boat out on the water. He left the buildings and jogged back over to the pier. A couple of men coming in from a cold day on the lake climbed out of their small fishing boats and onto the pier.

He looked out over the lake and spotted two boats still out there, heading away from the marina. He couldn't see them well enough to be able to tell who was manning the small boats. Except… Wait… It looked as though one boat was giving chase to the other one and appeared to be gaining on it.

Oh no.

That could very well be Chasey fleeing her pursuer.

Ben rushed up to one of the men who was tying up his boat. "Deputy US Marshal Ben Bradley. I need your boat. Someone's in danger out there." He pointed. "I need to help her before that man gets to her. Please, can I use your boat?"

The man nodded. "I'll go with you."

"Sir, this could be dangerous. A life is on the line. Wait here. I'll return your boat, one way or another."

The man lifted his hands and backed off. "I don't want any trouble. Do your job and save her. But you should know the tank is close to empty. It'll get you maybe halfway across the lake and that's it."

The man reversed his knot to untie the boat.

"Thank you." Halfway across—or at least

to Chasey—was all he needed. Ben hopped in and started the engine.

Silas rushed forward then stopped short of climbing into the boat with him. "Where are you going?"

"I'm going after those boats out there. Stay at the marina and remain vigilant. I can't be sure that that's her out there, so she might still be close by."

He steered from the pier then sped toward the boat chasing after Chasey—*if* that was Chasey. He prayed it wasn't, prayed that his instincts had been wrong—but he didn't think they were.

At least his boat seemed faster than the two on the lake.

Except after he accelerated, pushing the boat as fast at it would go, he realized it might not be fast enough.

The little fishing boat steadily traveled over the water. The sleet had turned to freezing rain and Chasey was even more grateful she'd grabbed a warmer jacket before she'd fled into the night, and into an early winter storm. She wouldn't last long out here without protection—and she might not last as it was, with this attacker on her trail.

God, I really can't believe this is happening. What did I do wrong?

She'd avoided social media and tried to dodge having her picture taken by her new friends if there was any chance it could end up online. She had even avoided having her photograph included on the staff and faculty web page of the college where she worked. She'd secretly shared with her boss, the dean, that she had a stalker and preferred to remain only a name without the picture. He'd readily agreed, letting her use just a cute graphic of books along with her name. But maybe even that had been too much. Maybe someone had gotten curious and looked deeply into her past. What could have tipped them off, though? She'd thought her new identity would hold up to scrutiny.

Or so Ben had told her.

Ben… Would he come for her?

She didn't see how he could make it in time because he could be anywhere. Escaping was all on her. She zeroed in on directing the boat across the small lake while feeling horribly aware every second that her pursuer was closing in.

She'd made a mistake in choosing to escape across the lake, after all, but she couldn't turn back now. One step at a time. One decision at a time. She had made this decision and had to see it through. In the meantime, she could plan how she'd hide once she reached the shore.

Chasey could just make out a small pier across the way. She focused on that and committed it to memory in case darkness fell before she reached it. She didn't want to get disoriented or she would be completely blind on the lake in these gray skies when night fell.

Lord, please let me get away. Please let me escape...again.

To think it had only been a year—a year—since the trial and she had already been located. She thought back to her uncle's words about retribution. Promising that, even from a prison cell, he would make her pay.

Well, he had to find her first.

Chasey had been the one to approach the authorities with information regarding her uncle after she'd discovered that he was a controlling member of an international terrorist organization. Prior to her report, no one had known about his insidious dealings because Chasey's uncle had spent a lifetime covering his tracks. He had a whole system of shell companies and secret paper trails through his textiles business that he used as a cover for his factories in several foreign countries. His reach spanned the globe. And he had kept Chasey under his thumb, under his watchful, intimidating eyes, as he'd forced her to work as his personal assistant.

Fear for her safety alone would not have been enough to keep her in line. He had other leverage.

Brighton. Her autistic brother.

When their mother had died while they were still children—Brighton only six and Chasey ten—they had become Uncle Theo's wards, and he'd taken good care of them both. There was no denying that he'd gotten Brighton the best care money could buy, or that Brighton had thrived.

Deciding to step forward as a witness—the only witness—who had seen first-hand her uncle's brutal and illegal activities, including murdering a man—had been a difficult decision. She'd feared for her life, and she'd feared for Brighton's life as well as his care.

Getting Brighton the best attention—equal to what her uncle could afford—had been one of her stipulations in coming forward as a witness. She and Brighton had been quickly whisked away to a safe house before charges had been filed.

To ensure he was safe and protected, she had insisted Brighton be put in a facility and disconnected from her. Placing the two of them together would make it too easy for them to be discovered if someone was searching. And Chasey had never doubted her uncle would search for her and make her pay for betraying him. She knew he'd always feared that she'd turn against him. It was why he'd kept her close. *Keep your friends close, but keep your enemies closer*, she'd often heard him say in meetings with his…um, "friends." He'd thought that with Brighton as leverage, he had her completely under this thumb.

But she'd found a way to escape.

And yet here she was on the run again.

She had no doubt that whoever was after her now was someone sent by her imprisoned uncle. And that meant he would not give up until he found her.

Chasey needed Ben's help again. But was there any chance he would show up in time?

She glanced over her shoulder to see the other boater closing in. Fear lodged in her chest and Chasey tried to catch her breath, but she couldn't seem to get enough oxygen.

Come on, come on, come on.

The boat's motor chugged, stuttered and then stopped completely.

Oh no, no, no. She tried to start the motor again to no avail. Out of gas? She found a lone paddle and considered paddling forward as fast as she could, but she knew she didn't have enough of a lead to reach the shore before he caught up to her. In the end, that wouldn't help her escape and would only be a waste of her energy.

And Chasey would need every bit of it to fight off her pursuer. Oh yeah, she would put up a fight. She could only hope that would be enough for her to survive until help came. *If* help came.

Fear built in her chest and her breaths came faster. White clouds puffed from her mouth. Gripping the paddle, holding it low so he wouldn't see, she turned to face off with the man who approached in a smaller fishing boat that he, too, had stolen.

He held a gun along with a grin as he sidled his boat up next to hers. "Get over here."

"Come and get me." Her heart hammered at the words. Would he kill her now?

"Suit yourself."

He hopped over and Chasey slammed him in the gut with the paddle. He grunted but wasn't deterred, grabbing her hair again, igniting pain. She held back her scream. What was with him grabbing her hair? This time she had a paddle instead of a lamp and she aimed for his private parts, shoving the wooden paddle toward him with all the force she could rally.

But he grabbed the paddle before she could make contact. A huge fail on her part.

The man had the nerve to laugh at her. He

was enjoying this? She shoved her leg behind him to try to trip him. If she could shove him over into the water, she would steal his boat and get away. But instead of stepping back, he yanked her around to see what was coming, thwarting her plan.

Another boat approached in the distance. Another of his goons?

Recognition slammed into her. Ben!

Her pursuer suddenly held the gun to her head. This was it then.

And Ben couldn't save her, after all.

THREE

Ben increased speed but he was already too late.

Chasey's attacker held a gun to her temple as he smirked at Ben. "She's dead already! Don't come any closer."

Ben shut off the motor, but the boat continued drifting closer, as he'd hoped, while he kept his gun at the ready at his side. "I'm a US Marshal. Put your weapon down. It's over." He said the words with all the authority he could muster, even though the man holding Chasey hostage had the upper hand. Ben hoped to quickly change that.

"It's not over until I say it's over," the man said.

What did the gunman want? Ben was almost afraid to ask. Was this the man who had killed Sheila? Had he gone after her because he'd been looking for Chasey all along? Ben wanted to get his hands on the murderer. But more than that, he wanted to protect Chasey. And if that meant he had to negotiate, he'd do it.

He kept his tone even but authoritative. "Just. Put. The gun. Down. And let her go. You can head to shore in the boat. All I want is the woman."

"You mean Kelly Cabot? Well, you can't have her. Nobody can have her."

So this man knew her true identity.

Her eyes held Ben's as his boat slowly continued drifted forward. Fear filled her gaze, and Ben's legs shook at the sight. But he couldn't fail her now. Somehow, he had to gain the advantage. Holding his weapon at his side, he didn't think the man had seen it yet. Ben fingered the trigger. Should he go ahead and shoot the man and risk hurting Chasey?

Would she die if he didn't take the chance?

Chasey's expression shifted and he suspected she might be trying to send him a message, but he couldn't figure it out and didn't want to clue in her abductor that she was trying to communicate. He soaked in everything he could without moving his gaze. Her hands were down at her sides and, sure enough, she fisted her hands and pointed. Still, he couldn't be sure what she was trying to say.

Maybe she was going to create a diversion. Yes. That would be something the woman he knew would do. He didn't nod or signal that he had understood her message, and hoped she would simply read in his eyes that he was on board with her no matter what.

Chasey dropped to her knees and grabbed the paddle then twisted around and punched the end into the man's most vulnerable parts. Gunfire rang out. Not his own. Had the man shot Chasey? Ben didn't have time to check—he had to spring into action to help Chasey, who was now grappling with her attacker.

He hopped over to the other boat, wrestling the man away from Chasey and disarming him—the weapon dropping into the lake. The man dove into the cold water rather than face off with Ben or be arrested.

Ben stared at the ripple left behind, debating whether to go after him. At the moment, he wasn't a danger to Chasey, but he was clearly a dangerous man, and might have been behind the attacks on the other witnesses. Ben needed answers...but overriding all of that was the need to keep Chasey safe.

"Are you going to shoot him?" she asked.

"No, of course not. He isn't armed."

"But he'll keep coming back for me."

That was a strong possibility. The sleet started coming down hard. "We need to get out of here."

"My boat is out of gas. It was sputtering there at the end just before he caught me."

"The one I borrowed, too. What about his?"

She shrugged. "We could try it."

Together they climbed over into the boat the man had used to pursue her in. "We'll need to make sure these boats are returned to the pier and their owners," he said. "I'll call someone to help with that later, but right now, we need to get you to safety."

Once they were in the gunman's boat, Chasey turned and looked at him, emotion thick in her eyes.

"Oh, Ben." She jumped into his arms, nearly bowling him over, and pressed her face against his shoulder.

He held her and at the same time watched the water. A few yards off, he thought he saw movement. The man swimming away? Darkness started closing in around them as they stood shivering in the cold rain.

"We have to get to shore." Ben glanced around them.

"I know, I know." She let go of him and stepped back. "Thank you. I didn't know if you'd get my message."

The boat that Chasey had been using was slowly sinking. The man must have inadvertently shot holes into it. "You're not hurt? He didn't shoot you or hurt you?"

"No. I think he wanted to take me somewhere. But I don't know." Tears choked her words. "I can't be sure."

Ben fought back the images of Sheila's bloodstained carpet. Had Ben's appearance prevented the man from killing Chasey? Or abducting her? All these thoughts ran through his mind as he steered the boat the rest of the way across the lake to a pier he'd spotted.

His job at WITSEC meant protecting his witnesses at all costs. Someone had breached the security measures in place, and he still didn't know how they'd done it. He would keep Chasey hidden from everyone for the moment until he was sure whom he could trust.

"We're not heading back?"

"I don't want to get caught on the lake in the dark. There's a pier up ahead." All of that was true, even if it wasn't the whole reason.

Ben took out his cell and contacted Silas to update him on what had happened. Ben suspected the attacker would swim to shore on the east side, so he told Silas to get the locals out there to pick him up. He ended the call, hoping they would catch the man.

"I had been heading across the lake without really knowing where I was going." She rubbed her arms. "I just knew I needed to get away and lose him. And I had almost made it, too."

Ben wrapped an arm around her and they stood close to keep warm as he directed the small boat toward the pier. Chasey continued to shiver next to him.

Maybe he could distract her. "You did well. You stayed alive until help could find you."

"Barely," she said. "If you hadn't arrived when you did, I'm not sure what would have happened."

Ben forced a reassuring tone. "You got away from him at your house—"

"You looked inside my house? How…how did you— I know I called you but I'm not sure how you got here so fast. I was surprised to see you on the lake, actually. Ben, why were you at my house? How did you know I was in trouble? What's happening?"

She'd figured it out pretty quickly. All his doubts and suspicions about what was going on around them crept back in. "Something happened with two of my other witnesses and I thought you might be next. I was already on the way to your house as soon as I realized you could be in danger."

"I see." She released a heavy sigh. "How did they find me?"

"I don't know." The boat approached the pier.

She held up the flashlight she found in the boat and started to flick it on before he pressed her hand down, stopping her. "No. I think we could give ourselves away. Let's use the dark to our advantage."

Her small gasp told him she understood the imminent danger. How he hated that her situation had deteriorated and she was now fleeing for her life.

"Even if you don't know for sure, you must have theories. How do you *think* they found me?"

"I don't know yet."

"How did you know I would be next?"

"It was just a hunch that you might be the target." He climbed onto the pier then offered his hand.

She grabbed it but scrambled up without needing much help from him. Her hands were like ice, and he wrapped both his around them. The sleet shifted to cold rain that continued to drench them.

"Target?" Her teeth chattered now.

Not good.

"Yes."

"As in, I'm the reason those other people were attacked? Whoever came after them was looking for me?"

"We don't know that yet," he hedged.

"But it's possible."

"...Maybe."

She huffed. "Is that all you're going to say?"

He didn't want to tell her about the murdered witness. "No. I'm going to say let's find someplace warm. There's a small shelter in the woods up ahead." He'd spotted it from across the lake but couldn't see it now through the shadow of the trees.

"I saw it earlier, too. Doesn't look like much. Not even a cabin."

"But it'll get us out of this cold rain." Holding her hand, he rushed with her across the short pier, the boards clattering as they stepped.

At the structure, he used the light from his cell to see and jiggled the knob. The door opened to reveal a small cozy space. He could barely make out a small cot and an old love seat. And a rocking chair and small table by the far wall.

"Don't turn on the lights," he said.

"Why not? How can we see?"

He covered his hand over his cell. "That should be enough. Sit there on that small sofa."

"Um... I don't know, Ben. What if there are spiders? Snakes?"

He chuckled. "This place looks like someone was recently here. I doubt there are too many pests around."

"I guess you're right. It smells like they cooked bacon this morning, and now we're trespassing."

"Desperate times. I'm sure whoever owns it will understand."

He ushered her over to the love seat and she eased onto it. Then he found a wool blanket folded at the end and draped it across her shoulders and lap.

"What about you?" Her teeth still chattered.

"Give me a second." Ben stepped to the window and watched the lake. He needed to make sure the man after her hadn't decided to follow them. He could have climbed into the remaining boat and escaped using the paddles. But he would let the local police worry about catching him.

Ben waited and watched. A silhouette against the night sky caught his attention. Someone hurried along the lake's shore.

Chasey's pursuer? The shadowy figure strode to the pier and then walked the length of it. It then crouched to look at the boat Ben and Chasey had left moments before.

When the man turned around, Ben recognized the US Marshals' insignia on his cap. Relief filled him that help had already arrived.

He moved to open the door then froze.

How? How had one of the marshals gotten here so fast?

Only Ben and Silas had been at the marina. This marshal hadn't crossed the lake, and he certainly couldn't have driven and arrived so quickly since the road curved away from the water, snaking through the foothills before coming back—if he'd even thought to drive this way when Ben had started across the lake. Something didn't add up. Was it possible their attacker earlier hadn't been acting alone? While one guy had gotten in a boat and pursued Chasey across the lake, had someone else gotten in a car and started the drive to this point, to cut her off if she managed to escape?

He turned off his cell and stood back in the shadows, watching. He couldn't see the man's face well enough to be able to tell if he recognized him.

"What's wrong?" Chasey whispered.

He appreciated she understood to keep her voice down. He lifted a finger to his lips. The man glanced around at the woods, his weapon pulled. He eyed the cabin, took a step or two in that direction, then appeared to change his mind and head back the way he'd come.

Ben slowly exhaled his relief. Chasey had quietly approached. He hadn't realized she stood so near until he heard her voice in his ear, felt the wisp of her breath against his skin. “What’s going on? That was a marshal, wasn’t it?”

Ben nodded. Then he turned to her and gripped her arms. “I don’t know who I can trust with your life, Chasey. I only know that you’re not safe.”

Chasey slid down in the seat of Ben’s car, hoping no one spotted her as Ben wasted no time driving them out of town. He’d taken both their cell phones and removed the batteries and SIM cards—taking no chances with being tracked—then returned what belonged to her.

Hugging herself as the heater kicked on, she wasn’t sure she would ever get warm again. The cold rain hadn’t stopped and she feared it was starting to turn into snow. Hiking through that mess on a cold, dark night had been horrible, especially given the day she’d had.

After the mysterious man had left, Ben had led her through the woods around the lake until they’d found an occupied house and knocked on the door. A retired veteran named Ted had been willing to take them back to the marina. Ben hadn’t wanted to wait around for his own people or the local law—and she was glad for that.

She didn’t know who to trust, and apparently neither did Ben.

He also asked Ted to please ensure that the boat left at the pier was returned to the marina as well as the other boat left on the lake. Ben then relayed to his co-worker one boat had sunk and they would need to pay for that. She was impressed by how hard he tried to cover all the bases and make sure he'd given back what he'd taken.

In that same vein, he had tried to leave Ted a cash gift for his help, which Ted had promptly refused. When they'd arrived at the marina, local police were already on scene and apparently combing the woods by the lake, searching for the man who had attacked her. But no US marshals were present, and she could see that Ben was oddly relieved by that. Based on what he'd said, she wasn't surprised. If multiple witnesses had been located, that meant the marshals' department couldn't be trusted. Not completely.

At least she could trust Ben. Of that, she could be sure, even if his team had been compromised. Chasey had never been more scared, because usually a person knew whom they could trust. Who the good guys were. And who the bad guys were.

As they drove off, she took in the last sights of the little shops and gas stations that made up the town she'd grown to love. Why had she thought she could create a permanent home and relax in her new identity? It had been foolish of her to think she could actually have some semblance of a home.

"Where are we going?" she finally asked when they'd driven for a while in silence. Ben hadn't offered any information. He seemed completely consumed with his thoughts—probably thinking through what had happened and what he needed to do next. The same thoughts were running through her mind, but she was willing to leave it in Ben's hands.

Ben would get her somewhere safe.

"First, we'll be heading to a contact who can put us in a different vehicle that won't easily be tracked."

"You really think that'll be a problem?"

"It could be, until we find out how information is being leaked. If someone could find your address, they shouldn't have any trouble finding the information on my car. I need someplace safe to think, and to keep you out of harm's way." A small chuckle escaped and he glanced her way, his cheeks dimpling.

Why'd he have to be so cute? She'd never gotten over those dimples. "What's so funny?"

"I don't know if I can get used to calling you Chasey. I keep trying, but it feels funny."

Ben and Chasey had grown close when she

was Kelly. But after the trial was over, she'd been quickly whisked away into her new identity and had little contact with Ben after that.

"Well, that's my new name, so it's best to keep calling me that." She pressed her head into the seat back, trying to talk herself into getting some sleep. This was going to be a long night and who knew when it would end. Or where.

"I know. I hadn't meant to suggest otherwise."

"Okay, Ben, now would be a good time for you to tell me what's really going on."

After blowing out a long breath, Ben relayed everything that had happened, starting exactly three days ago. "And that's all I know. I also know that you're my priority. I promise to keep you safe, Chasey. You don't need to worry so much as remain vigilant."

Vigilant.

The word Ben used to use all the time in the days leading up to her uncle's trial. This felt entirely too familiar. She crossed her arms, as if that could somehow keep her from being sucked up into feelings for Ben again.

"What about your other witnesses?" she asked.

"They're already being moved."

Chasey wrapped the news and the dry blanket Ben had handed her around herself as Ben cranked up the heat. She struggled to chase the chill away. What did it mean that Ben was here handling her personally? Was it just that he felt she was the main target—or was it something more? She stared out the window at the darkness, the occasional road signs or farmhouse lights.

What exactly had happened? Why were Ben's witnesses being targeted? She didn't want her thoughts to go there, but she could no longer ignore what caused dread to rise inside. "Is this about my uncle? Has he sent goons after all of these people because he's looking for me?"

"We don't know that yet. Let's not make assumptions. There are so many factors at play here that we just can't know for sure. But don't worry, we'll figure out who is behind it."

She nodded. She loved listening to Ben's voice. Something about it always comforted and reassured her. She just had to remember not to start to depend on it. Like before, he wouldn't be around for long. Once she was safe, he'd be gone again.

"If my uncle is behind it..." Who else would go to so much trouble? Most people in WITSEC had testified against someone with a lot of power. "He could be trying to throw you off with the attack on your other witnesses when all he wanted was me. But then that could be said about the other powerful people who might want revenge."

"I have to concede that point. Nothing is off the table." Ben didn't say more, leaving Chasey to her own imagination.

She stared straight ahead as the rain turned to snow and huge chunky flakes filled the ring of light cast by the headlights. How did Ben even see to drive? How far did they have to go to exchange vehicles?

Then it hit her… What about her brother? She hadn't considered that he might be in danger, as well, despite the protective measures she'd put in place. After her uncle's incarceration, she had petitioned for and received guardianship of Brighton. Although he was twenty, due to his autism, he seemed more like a child. A brilliant child, but one who couldn't live independently. He needed care and protection, which she'd tried to give him. But if her location had been leaked, did that mean his had been, too? The urge to call Brighton overwhelmed her, but Ben had said no phones, aside from the special burner phone he kept for just such an occasion. She could ask to use it, but she didn't think he'd let her, not right now when things were still so uncertain.

Whatever. All she knew was that she didn't have a way to contact Brighton. Chasey thought back to the battle she'd fought in her own home. What was Brighton doing, even at this moment?

Was he still safe? Tucked away in his bed, getting rest? Was he sitting up drinking hot chocolate by the fireplace? Chasey had to know. She had to be there with him and for him. Ever since she'd made the decision that they should live apart, she'd feared she had made a huge mistake. She'd wanted to make sure her severely autistic brother had excellent care—the absolute best. Holly House offered stability and safety like no other place she'd been able to find, even if their living arrangements were perhaps more restrictive than most. But given her and her brother's dangerous predicament, she had thought the arrangement as the best for him, at least until now.

The decisions she'd had to make had torn her apart and, right now, she ached to see her brother. "Ben, I'm worried about Brighton. Will you please take me to see my brother?"

Ben remained focused on the treacherous road ahead of them, but she trusted he'd heard her.

After a long pause, he said, "Let me think about it. We need to be certain that you're safe, and that no one can follow us. We wouldn't want to lead anyone to him, after all the trouble we've gone through to find the perfect place for him."

"I hadn't thought of that," she admitted, "but you're right. I wouldn't want him to be in danger, either. But I'm worried. Someone found me. What if whoever is behind this finds Brighton? I don't think he'd be able to defend himself physically."

Ben exhaled. "Brighton isn't exactly a witness. He's in a very tightly run facility, as well."

"You're the only one who knows where he is, right?"

"Yes."

"Is that a hard yes or a soft yes?"

"It's complicated. The database is kept secure."

Like the witnesses? Chasey heard what he didn't say, too—someone had found her and the others. But maybe Ben was right and her brother wasn't being targeted in the same way.

"I miss him." Tears slid down her cheeks. "I almost wish I had never given up my uncle."

"Believe it or not," Ben said, "I understand."

She sniffled. "I couldn't live like that anymore, standing by while so many terrible things happened. But at least then I could see Brighton. So now that you have to move me and give me a new identity, this time, I want you to put us together. I can't be separated from him any longer."

Ben sighed and reached across the console to squeeze her hand. An electric current spread up her arm and curled around her heart. Chasey bit the inside of her lip enough to guard herself against that old attraction she'd felt for the guy. During the time when he'd protected her before the trial, she'd fallen for him a little. Okay, well, a lot. And she'd thought he had felt the same way.

She closed her eyes and remembered their one and only kiss. A forbidden kiss, really—she was a witness and Ben, her protector. She had often thought maybe that alone had been what had drawn her to him—the drama and high tension of the moment—but in the year that she had lived in her new identity, she thought about Ben all the time.

Yeah, she'd flat fallen in love with him.

But given the circumstances, she could keep falling in love with him over and over, and he would just keep leaving her when he set her up with a new identity—a vicious cycle, that. No. There would never be a time or place to emotionally connect to Ben again. She had bigger problems—like staying alive.

And what about her brother? He wouldn't

have a clue if he was in danger. How could she keep him protected?

"Hey, Chasey. It's going to be okay. I'm here. I'm going to protect you. Brighton, too. I'm not going to leave your side until you're completely and utterly safe. No matter how long it takes."

Chasey wanted to believe him. Ben had never lied to her. She recalled his words to her a year ago, after the kiss…

I shouldn't have done that. We shouldn't do this. I can't follow through and be what you need, which is someone to love you and stay with you. I can never stay and be what you need me to be.

Pain stabbed through her heart at the memory.

Get over it, Chasey.

Ben was a man of his word. That meant he'd guard her with his life…but she couldn't trust him with her heart.

FOUR

Ben turned down a road until he found the car lot where he would meet an old family friend, C. J. Carlton. The guy owned the lot and had an older model vehicle for Ben to trade out. The Suburban wasn't equipped with GPS or any way for him to be tracked like his newer Volvo XC90.

Wearing a jacket, C.J. stood near to the running vehicle.

"C.J." Ben approached. "Thanks for meeting me."

"Glad to help a friend in need." C.J. thrust out his hand to shake Ben's. "I'm always here to assist if I can."

"And we're good on the funds?"

"Your brother said he will bring me the money tomorrow. I'm not worried about it. And, Ben, feel free to bring me the car when you're done. I understand these are strange circumstances. Don't worry, Reece didn't tell me anything I shouldn't know."

Reece was an investigator with the National Park Service, so he understood the need to keep the circle of information as tight as possible. He hadn't argued when Ben had called and said that he needed help, with no questions asked. But even though Ben hadn't shared any details, it probably wasn't hard for anyone to figure out he was trying to hide someone.

C.J. was smart, and very perceptive. It was a good thing he was also honest and loyal. Whatever he'd figured out, he'd keep to himself.

"I appreciate you more than you know. I don't want to lead danger to your door, though, so keep an eye out." Ben gestured toward his Volvo. "You should probably hide this away. I'm worried it could be tracked to you."

"I'll be fine. I'll park it up on the lot after I figure out how to switch the tracking off. I could do that for you if you could wait, but seems like you need to skedaddle."

"You would be correct." Ben and Chasey were definitely fleeing in the night. Normally he would usher her to a safe house—usually a specific pre-screened hotel—until he could establish her new identity. He'd spent his career preparing safe houses and knew where to go, where to stay. But given what had happened over the last seventy-two hours, he wouldn't trust any of those places. It would be safer for Chasey if he found a new place where no one would think to look for them.

"Thanks again for your help."

C.J. nodded. "The keys are in the Suburban and it's been running a few minutes now so it'll be warm."

"Great. I'll leave the keys in my SUV."

Ben approached the Volvo and opened the door for Chasey. She glanced up with sad, tired eyes. A pang of regret shot through his chest.

"Is it time to go?" she asked.

He nodded, anger and grief twisting in his gut that she was being put through this. That Ben had somehow missed the mark. Somehow, somewhere, he must have failed or else this would not be happening—to Chasey or to Sheila. His heart grieved for the witness who had lost her life. But he would have time to berate himself for failing her later. Right now, they needed to get moving. He ushered Chasey around to the passenger's side of the Suburban and opened the door for her.

She offered a small smile and her thanks as she climbed into the vehicle and buckled up.

Ben closed the door and waved at C.J. then made his way around to the driver's seat.

Ben hoped his brother also understood how

much Ben appreciated his help. But then, that was the kind of family he had. If Reece hadn't been around, then either their brother, Ryan, a detective for Maynor County, or sister, Katelyn, a former police officer turned private investigator, would have come to Ben's aide. No questions asked. No matter where Ben was working, his family would help. They had his back.

In considering Reece's help, Ben realized how close he was to home. He found new identities for the witnesses when they went into the program. New identities and a new life far from their previous lives. In Chasey's case, he'd placed her in a small town near where he grew up in the Mt. Shasta region of northern California.

Ben got into the Suburban and familiarized himself with this new-to-him vehicle. In fact, it wasn't only the vehicle that was new to him. Though fleeing the night, whisking a witness away and out of danger, wasn't new, this was the first time he'd felt on his own, unable to trust the rest of the department to help him. He couldn't call in backup or lean on departmental resources. Chasey's safety rested solely on his shoulders.

Comfortable with the vehicle, he started to shift it into gear, but dropped his hands in his lap. "Look. I'm so sorry this happened."

Chasey swung her head toward him. "It's not your fault, Ben. You don't need to apologize."

He wasn't so sure. He heard the exhaustion in her voice. Exhaustion from the long day, for sure, but more than that, he could see she was suffering from the psychological and emotional drain of being pursued and attacked.

"I hate that you're going through this. I know you're exhausted and probably hungry, too."

"You've always been thoughtful, Ben. But I know that you're going through this, too. You're going through it with me. I'm all right for now, and that, thanks to you."

Her voice was soft and sweet. He had often wondered how she was the niece of that jerk, Theo Dawson.

Ben put the Suburban in gear and headed out. Now he just had to find a secure location. Something different and not on the radar of any of his fellow marshals. Something no one could think to find.

Yeah, Ben, like you're going to find such a place.

He scraped a hand down his face. "So we're going off grid. As much as possible. It's not easy to do." And would be impossible for most. He kept cash on hand for emergencies, but it would only last so long. He had to figure things out and soon.

They only needed to stay off the grid until Ben knew who had been behind giving up his witnesses. Once he was certain the leak had been identified and plugged, he could rely on his colleagues again. But only when he was absolutely certain.

Because this had *inside job* written all over it.

If only he'd gotten a better look at the man who'd come to the pier. Thinking back, Ben wished he had taken the man down then and there, but he had been focused on keeping Chasey hidden and safe after a very close call.

He needed to contact Chief Calvin again to share these new thoughts, but didn't want to have that conversation in front of Chasey. He glanced her way. She'd fallen asleep—another reason why he should wait to make the call. He might wake her.

Ben kept driving on the lonely road as the temperatures continued to drop. He hoped the road wouldn't turn icy, but he couldn't stop until he found a place off the beaten path, far from where he'd left his trackable car behind. Maybe he would find somewhere on their way to Colorado to check on Chasey's brother. He knew she felt an urgent need to see Brighton, but for his part, Ben remained pretty confident in the young man's safety. Access to the assisted living facility was restrictive for protective reasons. It wasn't like someone could walk in and take Brighton away. He doubted anyone could find him. Brighton's location had not been kept on any WITSEC database, and the boy's trust from his mother funded his stay through covert channels.

And for that, Ben couldn't be more relieved.

Now if only he could be as confident in their own safety…

Chasey woke when bright lights shone in her eyes.

Where...where am I?

Heart pounding, she grabbed the armrests and glanced around. A gas station. She was at a gas station? Oh, that's right. Ben's getaway Suburban—that was the only way she could think about it. A getaway car.

Ben had obviously needed to buy gas. Rubbing her eyes, she glanced at the clock on the dash. Two in the morning? Where was Ben?

She twisted around and spotted him at the back of the vehicle by the gas pump. He was talking to someone on his burner cell, and he had his back to her. He suddenly turned to the side and glanced her way as if he'd sensed her watching.

He moved closer to the side of the vehicle and

stared through the window, looking over her like she was a precious treasure that he wouldn't leave unprotected. Though she blushed a little under his attention, she couldn't help feeling curious about his phone call. Who was he talking to at this hour?

Ben ended the call and stepped back to put away the nozzle. He then opened the driver's-side door and peeked inside. "You need a snack? Something to eat or drink? I'm sorry we didn't stop somewhere earlier, but you were sleeping and I figured I would drive until I had to stop for gas."

She nodded. "I need to use the little girl's room. Maybe you could grab some water for me." She thought to reach for her purse then remembered her attacker grabbing it off her shoulder back at the house.

She had the small emergency pouch strapped to her ankle that she wore when she was running—just a little cash, a spare credit card and her driver's license. But everything else was gone.

Ben watched her and seemed to understand her dilemma.

"Even if you had your wallet, I would advise not using bank cards or credit cards. I have cash and I'll get what you need. As soon as I can, I'll get you new identification. The works.

Okay?" He held her gaze, waiting for her to accept the truth.

"Okay. I just feel…" Chasey wasn't sure what she felt. Maybe *lost* was the right word. "I'm glad one of us is thinking. If you hadn't taken my cell phone, I probably would have turned it on and looked at it a few times by now, too."

"That's what I'm here for. Let's go in, then you can use the bathroom and pick out a snack," he said and closed his door.

She hopped out of the vehicle and they walked the short distance to the store entrance. She finished up in the women's restroom and then grabbed a few bags of nuts, an orange and some water. That would hold her over until they could get something more substantial.

Ben paid cash for her items along with a huge cup of coffee and a doughnut for himself. He winked at her and they grabbed their sacks from the counter.

They were just turning toward the exit when a masked man rushed through the door and pointed his gun at them.

Oh great. What now? She glanced to Ben for some signal but he never took his eyes off the masked man.

"You there, you're packing." The man pointed

his gun at Ben. “Put your hands on your head and don’t even think of reaching for your gun.”

“Look, man, we don’t want any trouble,” Ben said.

Standing so close to Ben, she could hear his increased breaths. Never good for law enforcement—special agent or deputy marshal—to be caught off guard, especially in Ben’s case. She just hoped he wouldn’t risk himself while trying to keep her safe.

“Ben, please…”

Ben placed his hands on his head. He probably planned to take action when the guy approached to take his gun from his holster. Chasey prepared herself to step out of the way.

“You.” The guy looked straight at her.

She ignored him, acting like she hadn’t heard him. She hadn’t expected his attention to turn to her. If he’d come in to rob the place, shouldn’t he be focusing on the man at the cash register?

“I’m talking to you, lady.”

She jerked her gaze to the masked man now, acknowledging that she understood, but she still said nothing.

“Now that I have your attention, remove your friend’s gun then very gently slide it over to me. Try any funny business and I’ll have to shoot.”

She tried to hide that she was shaking as she opened up Ben's jacket and reached to just beneath his arm, around behind his shoulder. His warm breath hit her cheek. She wished he could speak his thoughts into her mind.

What are you thinking, Ben?

Did he want her to hand the gun off to him and duck out of the way? Or did he want her to swing around and fire the gun into the man's chest?

After tugging the gun from Ben's holster, she backed away and flicked her gaze to his, holding it for a mere heartbeat before turning around.

"Eh, eh, eh… Dangle it between your fingers, honey, and trot it on over to me."

"I thought you wanted me to slide it over to you."

"I changed my mind."

Boy what she wouldn't give to give this—

"I see you're thinking about it. You want to hurt me real bad. I see it in your eyes. But you don't want any trouble, do you? I don't want any trouble, either," he said.

Could have fooled her, but she bit back her retort.

She held the weapon out at arm's length when she was close enough that he could reach it. *God, please let the cashier get control of this situation.* Call the police. Something. Ben didn't have his gun anymore.

Before she could react, the man yanked her forward and twisted her around. He held the gun to her head and started backing out of the store.

Twice in one day now, she'd had a gun pressed against her temple. Really?

"Wait!" Ben started forward.

The attacker tightened his arm around her throat. "Don't even think about it. You take one step out of this store and I'll kill all of you, starting with her. Get on the floor." Slowly, Ben complied. "And you—" he directed his words to the cashier "—you've got twenty seconds to empty that register and put the cash on the counter. Then come around from behind the counter and get on the floor. If I see that you have a gun on you, I'll blast a hole through you."

This was just an armed robbery and had nothing at all to do with someone after her.

The cashier nodded vigorously and opened the register after three tries. He pulled all the bills out and stacked them on the counter, then lifted his hands above his head so his cooperation wouldn't be questioned. He hurried around the counter and got on the floor, lying flat next to Ben. Hope drained from Chasey.

The man in the mask dragged her out of the store—without taking the cash, she noticed—and she couldn't help it.

Chasey screamed.

FIVE

Ben never took his eyes off the masked man as he dragged Chasey out of the store at gunpoint. From where Ben was positioned, he couldn't see the man's vehicle. He could only see the back of the Suburban at the gas pump as he looked through the glass-doored entrance to the store.

Chasey's scream had reached to his bones, pierced through his heart. He should have been more vigilant. What was wrong with him? He could berate himself later. Now he had to think. To act.

But he couldn't move. Not yet. The man who'd taken her continued watching Ben as if he sensed that at any moment he would spring up from the floor and attack. His muscles were coiled and waiting for that moment.

"You have an exit out back, don't you?" He mumbled the words to the other man on the floor in case the watching masked man could read lips.

"Yes," the cashier said. "What are you thinking? What can I do to help? I should have done something more—"

Ben was already moving. The masked man had disappeared from his sight, which meant he could no longer see Ben. That gave him the opening to get moving, but it also meant that Ben could no longer see Chasey, or where the man was taking her. What he was doing with her. If he didn't get eyes back on them soon, the man might succeed in dragging Chasey away, and Ben would have no idea where to find them.

He dashed for the back of the store, toward the red-glowing exit sign, and stepped out into the cold, dark night, taking care to let the door ease closed rather than let it slam shut. The sound would alert the masked man. Heart racing, Ben hurried along the back and then the side of the building until he could peek around the corner to the front.

The man had opened the trunk of his four-door sedan and, while pressing a gun under Chasey's chin, was attempting to force her to climb inside. Ben couldn't let him drive off with Chasey or she would be lost to him forever. Her life could very well be forfeit.

He'd already failed her monumentally. This never should have happened.

Ben knew to never let his guard down. Just like he knew not to let Chasey distract him so much that he forgot to pay attention to anything else.

He gulped air. It was now or never.

He had this one chance to save her.

He crept forward, willing the masked man to remain distracted by Chasey, who had been pushed into the trunk but was still putting up quite a fight, keeping her kidnapper from closing the trunk on her. She kicked out, making solid impact against her captor's chest, and the man—clearly angry and frustrated—lifted the gun as if he was going to hit her in the head.

Ben rushed forward and grabbed the man's arm from behind, calling on all of his training and experience to disarm him. At the same moment, the cashier burst from the storefront and pointed his shotgun at their attacker.

The masked man lifted his hands. Ben retrieved his weapon from the man's pocket and chambered a round before holding it up, aimed. "You won't be needing this anymore," he explained. "You're about to be locked up."

He glanced at the cashier, who nodded. "That's right. I called the police. They'll be here any minute."

"On the ground," Ben said.

"What? I'm not getting on the ground."

"Oh, you're getting on the ground." Chasey climbed from the trunk. "You're getting on the ground so we can restrain you or I'm going to kick you and you're not going to like where."

The man seemed to consider her threat, as if wondering if she'd really go through with it. The determined look on her face told him all he needed to know. He got on his knees then his stomach and placed his hands behind his head as if he'd had some practice with being arrested.

Sirens grew louder.

While Ben was glad for the police, he wasn't making any headway with his plan to protect a witness. He checked the man's pockets to see if he could find any identification, but there was nothing on him. Ben memorized the license plate.

Chasey looked at Ben and he thought he could read the question in her eyes. Should they stay and wait for the police? Ben had been all about avoiding encounters that could give her location or identity away. Even law enforcement couldn't be trusted, not completely. Not when it took only one turncoat to leak life-or-death information. But in this instance, they had no choice but to remain. The police were already too close, and they'd draw too much attention and suspicion if they tried to run.

He could only hope that the police finished with them quickly. Maybe he could gain distance and find a place to hide before Chasey's pursuer somehow got wind of their trouble tonight.

He wished that the attack on his witness was over and done with. That she wasn't a pursued target. But instinct told him otherwise. And if someone was able to track them to this gas station, that someone must be watching them very closely—closely enough to potentially learn the trajectory and their path.

Lights flashing and sirens wailing, both a highway patrol car and a sheriff's office vehicle sped into the gas station parking lot and simultaneously braked to a stop. Law enforcement officers jumped out of the vehicles and held their weapons up—not surprising, considering Ben was holding a handgun and the cashier had a shotgun. Not wanting to spook anyone, Ben lowered his weapon to the ground.

"That's the man right there." The cashier hadn't put away his shotgun. "He held us at gunpoint and tried to stuff this lady in the trunk of his car."

The deputy quickly handcuffed and ushered the attacker into the back of the county vehicle.

Ben and Chasey both gave their statements to the deputy and the Nevada state trooper. The deputy taking Ben's statement eyed his credentials and glanced up at him.

"What are you doing out this way so late at night?" He glanced between Ben and Chasey.

"Traveling," Ben said and crossed his arms.

The officer wrote in his notepad but said nothing regarding Ben's response. He handed their identification back to them. "All right, you can go now. We'll contact you if we have more questions. But thank you for what you did—it sounds like you were a hero tonight."

If only the officer knew just how not like a hero Ben felt. If he'd been more vigilant, more careful, more attentive to something other than the beautiful woman by his side, maybe he could have halted this whole situation before it began.

"The cashier deserves credit, too. If anything, we messed up by letting that guy catch us off guard."

"It happens," the deputy said. "But hang on to the fact that it all worked out in the end and that no one was hurt." He left them and walked into the store.

Looking over, Ben saw that the trooper was in his own vehicle talking on his radio.

Most likely, he was just reporting back to the

station. Most likely, it was completely innocent and nothing suspicious at all. But maybe, just maybe, he was talking to someone willing to pay handsomely for news of Chasey's whereabouts. Maybe it wasn't safe for them to stay a moment longer.

Ben turned to Chasey. As rushed as he felt, he still had the urge to catch her up in his arms. He wanted to comfort her and calm her nerves. But to his surprise, though he expected her to collapse after nearly being abducted, strength shone in her gaze and demeanor.

"Are you ready to go?" he asked.

"I think you forgot your coffee." She smiled.

He took her hand. "I just want to get out of here. With all the adrenaline I've got pumping through me right now, I don't need coffee anymore."

But as he climbed into the Suburban, the cashier came rushing out with their snacks, and a new and freshly poured cup of coffee for Ben.

Surprised, Ben grinned. "Thank you."

"Keep up the good work. You two have a safe drive. I'll be talking about this for days."

Ben groaned inside. *Please don't.*

Ben suddenly pictured the nightmare scenario of security cameras with their images and reports of the incident going viral. He needed to get Chief Calvin on that. He'd been leaving a message for the chief just before they'd gone inside, when Chasey had woken up while he was refilling the tank. He supposed it was time to leave another message now.

"I need to make a call," he explained.

"Sure thing." The cashier waved goodbye and rushed back inside where it was warm.

Ben called his chief, who answered immediately.

"I got your cryptic message. Where are you?"

Ben glanced at Chasey. He hadn't wanted to have this conversation in front of her. "I'm driving." He shifted into gear, eager to leave the gas station. "I saw the man who was after Chasey, and fought with him on the lake."

"Did you get a good look?"

"Yes, of course, but I didn't get a picture."

"We need you to work with an artist for a composite sketch."

"I understand that, but I don't feel comfortable coming back. Not yet. I think there's an inside man."

The chief sighed. "I agree that's a possibility. Getting hold of your list of witnesses would be no easy task. We're looking at all angles on this end to see who could have accessed the database, and we're not doing it alone. I'm in conversations with half a dozen different agencies to try to get to the bottom of this." Besides Ben, no one knew the details of his witnesses—their new identities and addresses—unless they got into the database. The US Marshals Service had set up the system decades before. It was the only way to ensure the safety of countless witnesses dependent on their protection against the organized crime element bent on retaliation. But no system was perfect.

"There's something more. When I helped Chasey escape, I saw a man dressed in a deputy marshal uniform. I didn't recognize him, but he was somewhere he shouldn't have been. Almost as if he was already in position, waiting for her. None of the men I took with me could have gotten there that fast. The only one who knew Chasey was out on the water was Silas, and that man definitely wasn't him."

"You're sure you're not mistaken? One of the other men could have got wind you needed help and was covering all the bases."

"It was dark and I didn't get a good look at him, but from what little I saw, he wasn't someone I recognized." Was he even a deputy marshal or simply disguised as one?

"Maybe I can line someone up for a virtual sketch session. Where are you now? What's your plan?"

"I'm going off grid with Chasey. Given how this thing has played out, I suggest the rest of my witnesses be kept in safe houses before being permanently reassigned to new locations."

The chief paused briefly before saying, "We're not moving anyone."

"What? I thought—"

"We've assigned a security detail to each of the witnesses you placed. There are only three more we need to be concerned with."

Ben ground his molars. "Fine. I'm personally handling Chasey. I have a theory this could be connected to her uncle. Someone's investing a lot into capturing her. I'll be in touch."

"You have my full permission to stay in protection mode—whatever it takes. Just keep in touch. Think about getting us a sketch—that could help the search."

"Yes. I'll call you with updates."

He ended the call before his chief could say more. Though he could feel Chasey's eyes on him, Ben stared at the long road ahead, both literally and metaphorically. He wouldn't stop at a hotel to rest now. Staying anywhere near here would make them too vulnerable.

And as he continued driving, he had the feeling the target on Chasey's back had just grown even larger.

Chasey noticed when Ben passed yet another hotel on the long stretch of road. *Okay. Time to speak up.* "I thought we were going to stop to get some rest."

"Can't do that now. After the gas station incident, someone with connections could learn our whereabouts. From there, it would be easy for them to figure out that we're on this road headed east."

Whoever had attacked his witnesses obviously had connections that could reach even into the ranks of law enforcement. He could take no chances.

"But you can't keep driving all night, Ben. Why don't you let me drive for a while?"

The grim set of his jaw remained in place. "Maybe later. I'm fine for now."

She could see well enough that he wasn't going to sleep. He was wound tight, especially after the call with his boss. What did it all mean?

"*You* should get some rest, though," he said.

"Oh, I can't sleep after all the action." In which someone had tossed her in the trunk of a car. Chasey rubbed her arms and sank down into the seat. "I keep thinking about that. I can't believe it happened. What are the chances? I've never witnessed an armed robbery in my life, not even in New York. When the man first entered the store wearing a mask, I thought that he was someone who had come after me. That we'd been followed and found. Then I was confused that he wanted the money and then I decided that no, this was just a robbery."

"Let me guess, you're starting to second-guess that now."

"I mean, if the guy was there to rob the gas station, why not wait until we were gone and the cashier was alone? More people around just meant more ways that things could go wrong for him. Add to that, why take me? Why stuff me in the trunk? And there's another thing."

"What's that?"

"He asked the cashier for the money but then he didn't take it."

Ben was quiet a few moments and then finally responded. "I thought that was strange, too. I don't want to scare you, but I had wondered if this was about you and not a random convenience store robbery."

"So you kept it to yourself? Ben, we're in this together. Please, tell me what you're thinking."

He shook his head. "I don't have any answers, just theories. All I know is that I want to get you far away. I want us to get lost and, depending on the level of sophistication of whoever is after you, getting lost won't be easy."

"I heard you talking to your boss. If the list of your witnesses is kept so secure, then you're right that whoever was able to access them is smart and ruthless. Has connections. Maybe they can hack computers. Maybe they just have a truckload of money for bribes. I don't know. But if they're determined to keep coming after me or your other witnesses, then it's going to be hard to lose them."

Ben nodded, staring at the road. "Somehow, I also need to get my fingers on the pulse of what's going on with the investigation so I can help find the person, or group, behind going after my witnesses. Technically that's not my job, but indirectly it's a way to keep you safe. There are a lot more resources I can use to protect you—but only if I can trust the department not to leak your location."

"You should tell your boss to start looking at my uncle." Even though he was in prison, she sensed that she still wasn't truly safe from her uncle Theo. While she didn't understand the inner workings of prison life and communicating with the outside world, she had no doubt that her uncle had established a network both inside and outside the prison walls.

He could get to her if he wanted, so that's why she'd gone into WITSEC—so he couldn't retaliate because he wouldn't be able to find her. In a way, Theo Dawson was like a mob boss, heading up his own "family" and she had betrayed him. But what if he had found her now? It sure felt like that was the case.

"Oh, believe me, my boss is talking to multiple agencies to look into where the threat is coming from. But it's a delicate situation because we need to keep witnesses safe and not expose them any more than they already are. Tonight, you're my priority. I need to find a place where you can be safe."

"I trust you, Ben. You're good at what you do and I've never doubted that. I know you'll get us somewhere off the grid."

"So, we're heading east instead of north or south. Does that mean..." Tears of joy choked off her words.

"That we're heading to Holly House to check on your brother? That was my plan."

She closed her eyes in relief. She was absolutely dying to see Brighton.

"I can't wait to see him."

"We'll talk about it, think it through, and make sure we're being cautious before we approach him. I don't want to lead anyone to him. But we'll get close, and then we'll look at what's happening with this security breach before we make a decision to see him. Brighton's in the safest possible place at the moment. Contacting him right now could be dangerous for him—and if we decide it is, then we'll need to keep our distance. Do you understand?"

"Yes. I would never want to bring harm to him. I've done enough by turning on my uncle." Rubbing her arms, she stared out into the silvery moonlit landscape of the desert.

Lord, please keep my brother safe. And thank You for sending Ben to save me back at the lake. And please help me not to fall for him again. Not to get hurt.

The more time she spent with Ben, the greater the danger of having her heart broken again. Getting across Nevada and then Utah would take a couple of days, even if they drove straight through. Spending all that time with him, never leaving his side, would she be able to maintain any kind of emotional distance? She just wasn't sure. She'd have to try to stay focused on her brother.

"Will they put a security detail on Brighton to keep him safe?"

"I'll call my chief back and ask. But we already know Holly House is well equipped with security and it isn't easy to get into or out of."

Ben grabbed Chasey's hand and squeezed, but said nothing more to reassure her.

Because, really, what could he say?

SIX

The sky turned gray with early morning light as they approached the outskirts of Salt Lake City, Utah. They'd made it through the rest of the night without anyone following them along the long stretch of highway, with only a few more stops for gas.

Ben should feel relieved but he didn't. From Salt Lake, it was another seven or so hours on the road, at least, to Denver where Brighton lived. And that was only if the weather cooperated. If they hit snow in the mountains, it could slow them down or potentially stop them altogether.

Am I making the right decision?

Was driving to the Holly House the best use of their time?

Was he only putting both Chasey and Brighton in danger? Should he risk a flight to Denver? No, definitely not. Whoever was after Chasey might be monitoring the airlines. It would certainly be easier watching the airports than watching all of the roads, which meant the roads were the safest place for them right now.

A horn honked and Ben opened his eyes to see the grill of a vehicle coming right for him. His heart jumped to his throat.

"Ben!" Chasey shouted.

He swerved back into his lane and caught his breath. Pushed his heart back into his chest. But his pulse still pounded violently. He'd...he'd fallen asleep? He had to do better than this. So much better or he would end up getting them both killed.

"That's it," Chasey said. "I'm driving now."

"You're in no better shape than I am." Ben exhaled, letting the rush of adrenaline drain out of him. "We're stopping."

"What? In Salt Lake?"

"It should be fine. There're a lot of people here and we can get lost in the crowd."

"If they know which direction we're headed, then there are only so many state highways we could take from that gas station, and Salt Lake is an obvious place to stop," she said. "I don't... I don't want them to find us again."

"We don't have a choice." He didn't like to admit it, but it was true. "I'll find a place off the beaten path." He turned into another gas station and pulled up to the pumps.

He sensed her growing anxiety and added, "Don't worry. Once we get some rest, we'll drive straight through to see your brother."

They'd both been through so much in the last day that it was weighing on them, exacting a price. They were both drained and Ben was forced to admit they couldn't go any farther tonight.

Her lips cracked into a brilliant smile, which completely surprised him, but then again, news of going to see Brighton had put it on her face. That smile reached all the way to her warm hazel eyes. Ben's heart jumped around inside. He would love for that smile to be for him.

He pushed that unbidden thought deep down and out of the way.

"I hope he's safe," she said. "He has to be. But I can't help but worry, and I miss him." The smile fell from her lips and she looked at the gas station.

No doubt she was remembering what they'd gone through only a few hours ago.

"I'll gas up and then we'll find a hotel. We can order takeout. Are you okay waiting to get something to eat?"

"Sure. I still have the snacks from the other place." She lifted the bag.

Neither of them had eaten after that terrifying experience, though Ben had downed the coffee. A lot of good that had done. He'd still fallen asleep at the wheel.

Ben counted the cash in his pocket. Really, he would have benefitted from a vehicle that was less of a gas guzzler, but that had been the trade-off he'd made. He'd needed something safe, anonymous and without any trackable software installed, that C.J. could provide right away. The old Suburban had been the best option, but that didn't mean it was without its drawbacks. At this rate, he'd run through his stash of money very quickly. He could only hope that he'd have other resources to draw on when that happened. As soon as they checked into a hotel, Ben would contact Chief Calvin to find out if he had learned who had been behind the attacks.

Chasey rested her head against the seat back, trusting Ben with her life. He hesitated mentioning Brighton to his chief. If his supervisor sent someone to watch out for Brighton, then their inside man might be able to learn where Brighton had gone. If not, Brighton wouldn't be as well protected. But only Ben and Chasey, Brighton's sister and guardian, would know his whereabouts. Ben had no choice but to trust that the facility was secure and that Brighton remained well hidden.

He dashed inside the convenience store and

left enough bills for the gas. "Keep the change." Then hurried back to the Suburban.

He found Chasey snacking on Doritos.

"I thought you were going to wait to eat. I don't want you to ruin your breakfast."

"Breakfast?" She arched a brow. "This is dinner, after which I'm going to crash, thank you very much. Maybe we can do a late lunch. But, Ben, what about clothes? Toiletries? I've got…nothing."

"We'll get checked in and then I can pick up what we need." And somehow keep a low profile while protecting her.

He would just have to remain vigilant—more vigilant that he'd already been.

One thing for certain, Ben needed a few hours' rest so he could think clearly. He had the sense that he was missing something important. He steered from the gas station and drove around the city until he found them a motel off the beaten path, as he'd promised. Then he paid cash for two connecting rooms to give Chasey privacy while keeping her safe.

After ushering them into their adjoining rooms, Ben parked the Suburban across the street behind a shopping strip mall. On the off chance that someone was tracking the vehicle, having some distance from it would give him a head start in getting away. He hoped. He had a lot of tricks up his sleeves, but if there truly was an inside man, that person would also know many of the same tricks, and could already be one or many steps ahead of Ben.

Their rooms were at the back of the hotel, blocked from the parking lot's view behind a copse of trees. There were pros and cons to that, but Ben chose to take advantage of the trees. He jogged across the street and entered his room. He found Chasey snoring on the bed in hers.

Before he slept, he needed to check in with the chief. Ben checked the locks on the door in Chasey's room, and mostly closed the door between their rooms, leaving it open a crack. He didn't want to wake her, so he stepped outside his room, leaving the door partially open, as well. He leaned against the wall and observed their surroundings. If he angled just right he could catch a glimpse of the parking lot across the street. He saw no familiar vehicles, except the Suburban. No snipers could position themselves to take a shot at her.

He moved to stand in the trees where he could both watch his surroundings and engage in a private conversation.

Before his brain was too fried, he called his chief.

"Bradley. I've been waiting for your call."

Ben didn't like the sound of the chief's tone, and dread filled his gut. "What's happened?"

"Your brother contacted us because he's worried about you. Someone put C. J. Carlton in the hospital."

"What? When did that happen?"

"Sometime last night. Reece wasn't able to contact you to warn you, but he believes C.J. was beaten to force him to give up information about the vehicle you took from the lot."

Not good. "Is he going to be okay?"

"I have someone checking on him."

"Even if they know the vehicle, it doesn't mean they can find us."

"It's your decision whether or not you want to ditch the Suburban."

"Thank you for keeping me informed."

He wanted to hang his head to absorb the news but instead remained alert. He'd made the right decision parking the Suburban behind a strip mall. Now he wondered if he would just have to leave it and secure entirely new transportation—somehow. With barely any money. People like C.J. didn't exist on every corner.

"What of the other witnesses?"

"So far, so good."

"That makes me question why someone is so aggressively pursuing Chasey. It's sounding more and more like she was the main target all along."

"I hear you and we're looking into possible ties with her uncle, but that can take a while."

"What about the man who attacked us at the gas station? The way that went down seemed strange. He claimed he wanted to rob the place, but he seemed much more interested in capturing Chasey. Who is he?" Ben had not found ID on him.

"I have someone looking into him. Nothing to report yet. And I personally questioned everyone in our offices last night, and everyone is accounted for. I don't know who the marshal you claimed you saw is."

"Claimed, I saw? Chief, I *know* what I saw—even if I can't be sure that the man was in a uniform that he earned rather than one he bought or stole. And what about the man who went into the lake? Were the locals about to grab him?"

"No. And…there's something else."

Ben sighed. "What is it?"

"Your Volvo is toast."

"What do you mean?"

"Someone set it on fire at the car lot. You've made someone very angry." Chief Calvin blew out a breath. "By taking Chasey to safety and thwarting her attempted murder or abduction, you've made an enemy, Ben."

"It wouldn't be the first time."

"I'd say let's hope it's the last, but that doesn't sound exactly right, either."

Though the comment might have elicited a chuckle on another day, Ben couldn't bring himself to laugh. "I'll contact you again soon."

Ben ended the call, but his chief's words still ricocheted around in his brain.

You've made an enemy, Ben.

Ben had been leaning so heavily on thinking that Chasey's uncle was behind the attacks on Ben's witnesses in a search for his niece, he hadn't thought about the attacks being about *him.*

If this really was about Ben, he was doing Chasey no favors by trying to protect her personally. She'd be safer the farther she got from him...

A fierce pounding grew louder in his head. He went back into his room and laid on the bed, hoping he could sleep because he had a long drive ahead. But he knew that he wouldn't be able to sleep.

What do I do, Lord?

Ben made one more call on his cell then closed his eyes.

Chasey curled under the covers and positioned the pillow over her head. Though it blocked out daylight, it barely muffled the noise of the housekeeper vacuuming in the room next door. Or the traffic along the highway or all the other activity that came with the day. Too bad that the world seemed intent on waking her up. She would love to keep sleeping so she could forget the dangerous predicament she was in.

Growling, she threw off the pillow and sat up.

Bright white from the snow outside cut through the cracks in the curtains. Chasey stretched and yawned as she listened to her stomach growl.

Brighton was only another day of driving away. Less than a day—seven hours, Ben had said. She glanced at the clock. No wonder she was hungry. It was nearing noon. Ben had explained he'd paid for two days so they could get the rest they needed without worrying about checking out before noon. But the sooner they were underway, the faster they would see Brighton. She was eager to get going—but only if Ben was ready to head out, too. If he was still sleeping, she knew she should let him rest. He'd need to be at his best to make the drive and stay on top of protecting her.

Protecting them.

She couldn't shake the sense that Brighton

needed to be protected, too. That this was about more than witnesses or even retaliation.

Uncle, what are you up to?

Knowing she wouldn't be able to fall back to sleep because she was eager to see her brother, she slipped from bed and eyed the shower.

Oh. That's right. She had nothing to change into. Oh well, at least she could freshen up a little. At the sink she washed her face and, in the mirror, she noticed a plastic bag on the floor near the small table by the window. She'd missed that when she'd gotten out of bed.

She rushed over and opened the bag. Seeing it contained clothes, she eagerly dumped them on the bed. When did he do this? Chasey lifted the items—jeans, sweats and a couple of T-shirts. Enough to get her through until this was over, or until she had the opportunity to buy her own things. Also included was a small bag of toiletries. How thoughtful.

Of course, she'd always known that about Ben. During the time she'd spent living out of a hotel while she'd waited for trial, Ben and a couple of other marshals—Lisa and Natalie—had been stuck in the room with her. They had been assigned to protect her; she'd been terrified of reprisal or murder to keep her from testifying against her uncle. She'd been the only witness against him.

Oddly enough, Ben had been much more attuned to her needs, much more thoughtful, in making sure she was comfortable and happy and lacked for nothing, than the two female deputies. Later, she'd hoped that might have had more to do with his feelings for her—though she'd never been sure if she was right about that or just seeing what she wanted to see.

Whether or not he had fallen for her as she had for him, they'd both known he would never stay with her or commit to her. She would do well now to remember what happened before, how much he'd hurt her, and not let Ben's kindness get to her again.

Chasey readied for the day. It felt good to be clean and dressed in clothes she hadn't been jogging in the day before or had fought with two different men in while fleeing through the night.

Slumping to the bed, she thought through everything she'd undergone the previous day—and then earlier than that. Yesterday had been the most dramatic day of her life… But back before the trial, before she'd turned in her uncle, she'd endured living in fear when her eyes were opened to the kinds of business activities he'd participated in. The dangerous clientele he worked with. She'd only been "free" for this past year, living under a new identity. Had only started to believe she could have a chance at a new life the last few weeks. Still that new life hadn't included Brighton. They'd separated because she believed her uncle or anyone working for him would have a more difficult time finding them if they were apart rather than together. In the end, that hadn't mattered and she had been found anyway.

Once she and Brighton were together again, and she hoped that would be soon, she would never again be separated from him.

When the tears surged, Chasey pressed her face into her hands and prayed.

Lord, how long do I have to go through this? Haven't I endured enough? Please protect us from whoever is pursuing us. Please keep us safe from the wicked men after us. And please, please, hide Brighton in the shadow of Your wings.

A hand gently pressed against her back and she started, relaxing when she saw that it was only Ben. He eased next to her on the edge of the bed, smelling of soap and dressed in new duds, too.

"Are you all right?" He grimaced and gave an apologetic shrug. "Sorry, that was a dumb question."

She grabbed his hand in both of hers and squeezed. "I'm as good as I can be at the moment. Thank you so much for the clothes. How and when did you get them?"

He smiled. "You're very welcome. I couldn't sleep, so I ran over to the store and grabbed the few items that we needed. After I took care of that, I slept for a while."

His laugh warmed her inside, and the usual warning signals went off in her head. But Ben's charm was entirely addicting, and even though she knew it would be safer, she didn't really want to resist his magnetism. He made a great marshal, but she couldn't help but think that with his charm and confidence, he could have excelled at so many different occupations.

"Why did you become a deputy marshal?" she asked.

Ben's expression told her that her question surprised him. He tucked some of her still-wet hair behind her ear. Did he realize that his touch sent tingles over her?

He got up from where he sat next to her and moved to glance cautiously out the window. "I don't know. I guess maybe because I grew up in a family of law enforcement. My parents, older brothers and one sister are all cops or special agents, or in Katelyn's case, a private investigator, but she was a cop first. I guess I just never considered doing anything else. I ended up applying to the US Marshals Service."

"You love your job, don't you?" Chasey wasn't sure why she'd asked the question when she knew the answer was yes. Maybe it was because she still had foolish dreams of the two of them staying together. But that wouldn't be possible as long as he was a marshal. He'd have to give that up to get a new identity and be placed with her. Unless he was willing to leave the marshals' service, the job would always stand in the way of a future between them.

Ben didn't answer but instead frowned as he stared out the window. "Gather your things. We have to leave. Now."

His tone left no doubt that they were once again in immediate danger.

SEVEN

Ben watched Chasey fix her small pouch against her ankle again then gather her things to stuff everything into a bag. Ben hadn't thought about buying a duffel. During his time as a deputy US marshal, in which he protected dozens of witnesses and helped move them into new identities, he'd never had to resort to such extreme measures, and living out of plastic bags brought that home.

Was he overreacting because the witness in jeopardy was Chasey? Maybe he should accept help from other deputies, like Silas. But until he knew who was behind Sheila Redgrave's murder and the attacks on Susan Lively, Chasey and now C. J. Carlton, Ben would lie low with Chasey.

No one should be tracking them anyway.

But despite Ben's best efforts, someone obviously had been following them. He'd taken all possible precautions and still they had been found. That was the only way to explain that someone had circled the strip mall and slowed near his Suburban. The white pickup had slowly driven off only to return twenty minutes later.

Was it someone who had attacked them before? Ben hadn't caught his face. But he didn't need to see a face to know he was in trouble.

They were onto him. Whoever they—he or she—actually was.

"Ben." Chasey's voice pulled him from the window.

She lifted a plastic bag in each hand. "Dirty clothes and clean clothes plus toiletries. I'm ready."

Oh. "Just give me a minute—I need to make a phone call."

He'd deliberated about his next move, the advantages and disadvantages it would bring. If he called his chief and had the local cops or the deputy marshals swarm in on this guy, their location and movement would be exposed. But whoever was behind this likely already knew, given the way that pickup was circling the Suburban.

He could no longer use the Suburban he'd gotten from C.J. He ground his teeth, hating that all the driving hadn't bought them even a day of anonymity, and called his chief.

The man answered immediately. “Bradley. What’s the latest?”

“We have a tail, Chief. Get this guy and you may have the man behind the murder and attacks. Or if not, you could at least get some answers.” Ben gave the chief the license plate, the truck make and model, and where it was located.

“Got it,” Chief Calvin said. “What are you going to do next, Bradley? Scratch that. This isn’t a secure line. Check in with me in a few hours.”

“Will do.”

Chasey followed Ben around his room as he grabbed the few items he had with him.

Two plastic sacks over his shoulder, he was ready to go.

Chasey looked at him. “What are we doing now? I couldn’t help but hear what you told your boss.”

Ben was glad for the trees because he couldn’t see the pickup parked across the street. If he couldn’t see it, then neither could he and Chasey be seen.

“We’re getting out of this place. Zip up your jacket, because we’re walking from here.”

“Walking? But—”

He cracked a grin. “It’s not far. We’ll wait for a cab.”

"And then what, Ben? What's going on? We're not driving the Suburban?"

"It's compromised."

"I can't believe this. What are we going to do? It's like, no matter what we do or where we go, someone is right on our heels."

Ben took a calming breath. He needed Chasey to believe in him and trust him to protect her. To follow his every instruction.

"Stick close to me. I'll do a quick perimeter check to make sure we're clear to move. You found that knit cap I got you?"

"Yeah."

"Put that on. Tuck all your hair underneath. Let's look like other people while we grab that cab." Here came the risky move. "But I'm going to leave first, so it doesn't look like we're together. I'll call the room phone to let you know it's clear, and then you'll need to walk in the opposite direction toward the shopping mall. Head into the coffee shop at the far end. Remember, hair in hat—and head to the coffee shop. You got it?"

Her hazel eyes were wide as she listened to his instructions, then she slowly nodded. "I got it."

"Keep your head down. I don't want anyone to get a good look at your face." Ben glanced across the street and spotted a cop car pulling up next to the parked white pickup.

"Forget everything I just said. We're both leaving now."

She tucked her hair inside the hat and followed him through the open door. Together, they casually walked across the street and headed for the coffee shop at the far end of the strip mall. Ben was itching to get his hands on the man who had trailed them, but Chasey's safety came first and arresting someone wasn't part of his job.

Once outside, cold and snow whipped around them in a late-autumn snowstorm. Great. He hoped that didn't slow air travel.

"I know it feels like we need to hurry. To run. But let's move casually. Talk and laugh. We're just two people out shopping."

"Whatever you say, Ben. You've been through this a lot of times, I'm sure, so you know what you're doing."

And that was just it, he had never actually done this before. There had never been a need. Another police cruiser steered into the parking lot. He could only imagine what was happening now. Would they take the driver in for questioning? He sure hoped the chief could pull that off, and the marshals could talk to this guy. He would let his supervisor deal with it for now.

The chief had his back. When he sent him a picture of the man who had tailed them here in Salt Lake City, Ben would know whether or not it was the same guy.

If it was a different person, that would mean this wasn't over yet. Even if was the same person, it might not be over.

After waiting for a traffic light, Ben and Chasey could cross the street and hit the strip mall, leaving the hotel and the Suburban behind.

At the coffee shop, he tugged her inside and they ordered hot coffee and breakfast sandwiches. Their items in hand, Ben called for a cab, since he didn't have Uber on his burner phone anyway, and to stay as low-tech as possible. Sure, the cab driver might be able to identify them, but they would be long gone by the time that information was traced down. Anything he could do to obscure leaving a trackable trail would keep them safer.

Law enforcement had an abundance of tools available, but so did the bad guys.

Once in the cab, Ben asked for them to be driven to the airport. Chasey said nothing, but he saw the questions in her eyes. He gave her a look he hoped she interpreted to mean he was asking her to simply trust him—just a little longer. Talking about their plans in front of a cabbie who could then later be questioned by someone, wasn't a good idea.

Then again. "I hope we can make our flight to the Florida before this storm causes delays." He squeezed her hand.

"I can't wait to take our Caribbean cruise and get out of the cold weather."

Good. She understood.

The cabbie dropped them off at the departures terminal, and Ben tugged Chasey over to sit on a bench. He glanced at his watch and then his cell phone, hoping he wouldn't have to wait much longer for their ride.

The temperature was dropping, even as their exposure to danger was increasing.

Chasey was more confused than ever. She'd thought they had to avoid the airport—that it would be too easy to track their travel if they went via airplane. But she couldn't help the giddiness rolling through her at the possibility of reaching Denver that much sooner.

She missed Brighton, but she had the feeling that he *needed* her, too.

Oh, Lord, please let him just be all right.

And Brighton being all right might actually mean she should stay away. She was so confused about what was best.

Instead of going inside the airport, Ben remained outside, waiting near her bench as a string of cars dropped passengers off for their flights. He appeared wary and watching. Vigilant. She chewed on her lip to keep from smiling. He used that word so constantly, she felt like she could hear it even when he wasn't speaking at all. It wasn't exactly funny. So why did it make her smile? Then she caught him staring at her.

He was watching *her* instead of the human traffic coming and going.

Then those dimples split his cheeks. "You did great back there in the cab."

"Oh yeah? You liked that?" An image of her and Ben on a Caribbean cruise flicked through her mind. *Oh no. Not now. Not here.* She couldn't afford to daydream like that, especially when it came to Deputy US Marshal Ben Bradley.

He crossed his arms, which made him look much bulkier in the coat. "You picked up on the subterfuge quickly."

"Subterfuge? Are you telling me we *aren't* going on a cruise?"

A slight frown formed between his brows and he studied her as if trying to find the answer to some deeper question. Oh no, was she blushing? "I'm teasing, of course!"

Chasey had to look away.

For a moment, though, she imagined that Ben was having the same fantasy. The two of them together on a cruise. Happy. In love. Married. But that's where the dream died away. Ben could never commit like that, not when joining her in witness protection would mean giving up his career. She shook off the weirdness and forced herself to look at him. Act normal. Though, really, what was normal in this situation?

Smiling, she shook her head. "Now would be a good time to tell me what we're doing, since we're clearly not getting on a plane," Chasey said. "It feels like you're waiting on someone?"

"I'm not waiting on someone. *We're* waiting on someone."

"Funny. I'm obviously tied to you until this is over." She hadn't meant to say that out loud. It sounded too…final. "I still don't understand. Who do you even trust enough to tell them we're here?"

A woman rushed up to Ben, surprising Chasey.

"Danielle, what are you doing here?" Ben kept his voice low.

"I'm not alone," Danielle said. "Your brother is in the car. Let's talk inside the vehicle, where it's warm."

Danielle hurried away and left them to follow.

Ben glanced at Chasey, appearing a little confused, but Chasey's confusion was much greater. His brother was here? And who was this Danielle person? She kept close to Ben as they followed the beautiful woman to a car.

Ben opened the door to the back seat and gestured for Chasey to get in. She did, and he followed. Once they were settled, she turned her attention to the two people in the front seats. A man she assumed was Ben's brother, and Danielle.

His brother pulled away from the curb.

"Chasey, meet my brother Reece Bradley and his fiancée, Danielle Collins."

"It's nice to meet you," Chasey said.

"Reece, what's going on?" Ben asked.

"Like we agreed last night, I flew out to Salt Lake and rented you a car. Only, Danielle was the one who officially rented it. I didn't want anyone to be able to track you through me."

"You should have told us you needed luggage, Ben," Danielle said. "We could have brought that, as well."

"This is only a temporary situation," Ben explained to Danielle then quickly shifted back to his brother. "I don't want to put more people in danger, Reece."

Chasey assumed he was speaking of Danielle's involvement.

"This is the best way," Reece said as he continued to focus on the airport road, staying in the busy rush of other cars picking people up and dropping them off.

"But someone might see that you've flown out here, and track you this way."

"That's why I brought Danielle. It was her idea and, once I told her my plan, she insisted on being the one to rent the car in her name. So you can thank her."

"Thank you," Ben and Chasey said at the same time.

"I'm sorry you had to go through all the trouble to fly here," Ben said.

"You've never asked anything of me before," Reece said. "But you're in strange waters this time. It's no problem to help you. It goes without saying that you'd do the same for me."

"Ben, I owe you," Danielle said. "You did so much for me and my little girl."

"Little girl?" Chasey glanced between Ben and Danielle. This was a part of Ben she hadn't gotten to know last year. His personal life. Chasey was suddenly hit with the fact that she hadn't known Ben at all—other than his character. His background, his childhood, the names of family members—including, it would seem, nieces and nephews—were all a mystery.

"Danielle's little girl is the sweetest thing," he said. "If I remember correctly she's six now."

"That's right," Danielle said.

"Big blue eyes and curly blond hair," Ben said.

"Like her mother," Reece said.

"Where is she?" Ben asked.

"Mom's keeping her." Reece reached across the front console and took Danielle's hand.

Chasey caught a glimpse of a solitaire diamond on her wedding finger. The engagement ring—beautiful but not so huge to be gaudy. She decided she liked Danielle, what little she knew of her. Chasey noticed that Ben's gaze snagged on the diamond engagement ring, as well, not with curiosity like her, but with a quiet sort of contemplation.

What was he thinking?

"I'm assuming you guys are going back home," Ben said. "Flying back today. I've already asked you to endanger yourselves far too much. Keeping Chasey safe is *my* responsibility. I'll pay you back, Reece, I promise."

"First, you're my brother. I've always got your back, even when no one else does. More than that, we're both in law enforcement. I know as well as you do the risks of the job—but we do them anyway so we can keep people safe." He nodded at Chasey. "You've got someone you're watching out for, and you couldn't trust your own, so you had no choice but to ask for some outside help. I understand that."

"I want to be able to trust them but… I can't say more than that."

"And you don't have to," Reece said.

Reece, who'd appeared to be driving in a big circle, now entered the arrivals area. "Danielle and I are going to take off again, and leave you with the car."

"I told them I needed it for a couple of weeks," she added. "It can always be returned early."

Ben's expression told Chasey that, while he was grateful, he still felt terrible for needing to pull his brother into a dangerous situation like this. And not just his brother, his brother's fiancée.

Chasey reached across the seat, grabbed his hand and squeezed. He glanced her way and she offered him an affirming smile.

"I can't thank you enough, bro," Ben said.

Reece pulled up next to the curb. "Ben, we can stay if you think you need help. You're not in this alone unless you want to be."

"No, we're fine. Chief Calvin's got my back."

Reece nodded as Danielle stepped out of the vehicle. Reece remained, shifting to look Ben in the eye. "Where will you go?"

"As I mentioned last night, we need to get

to Chasey's brother to make sure he's safe. If I have any sense that he's also in danger, we'll take him out of there before hitting the road again to get somewhere safe."

"You always seem to have safe houses and, of course, hotels."

Ben shook his head. "I can't use any of it. I need someplace new."

"Do you have anything in mind?" Reece asked.

Ben glanced Chasey's way and gave her the oddest look. "Yes. Yes, I think I do."

With that, Ben got out, and Chasey followed his lead. They said their goodbyes to Reece and Danielle, keeping their actions as casual as possible, like they were simply dropping friends off at the airport.

Danielle and Reece pulled their packs from the trunk. They had planned for anything, it would seem.

Chasey watched them walk away, hand in hand, and…very clearly in love.

"Chasey." Ben's voice pulled her head around. He stood next to the front seat's passenger door. "You ready?"

She nodded and got into the car with Ben. After strapping in, she said, "It must be so nice to have family like that. People you can trust and lean on for anything." *Anything at all.*

Chasey had never had family like that—at least, not that she could recall. Memories of her parents were mostly hazy, and while she loved Brighton, he'd always been someone for her to shelter and protect rather than someone to lean on. And as for her uncle…well…no need to dwell on that.

Ben steered the vehicle away from the terminal and off the airport property. "I'm sorry for what happened to your family, and that your uncle turned out to be so bad, but you have Brighton, Chasey. And he's so fortunate to have a loving, caring sister like you. Once we get on top of what's happening and I get you settled with a new identity, things will calm down again before you know it. The next thing you know, you'll meet someone, fall in love and have a family of your own. I know you'll make a wonderful mother."

EIGHT

Oh brother.

He'd only meant to encourage her. He just hadn't meant to take it quite that far.

Why had he just kept going on and on, reassuring her that she would fall in love and have a family?

He'd seen the way she'd watched Reece and Danielle walk away, hand in hand. Obviously, they were meant for each other.

Ben had felt a sliver of jealousy, but not in a negative way. Good for Reece. Good for his brother. He couldn't be happier for all his siblings finding someone to share their lives with. Finding love.

He could understand Chasey feeling a little envy of that, as well, though he imagined that her real longing was to have grown up in a normal family. What she really wanted was to have those around she could trust. And as sad as it was that she'd never had that, he knew that there was, unfortunately, nothing to be done to change it. He couldn't erase her past or any of the terrible experiences she'd endured, losing her parents and then finding herself trapped in her uncle's sinister web. But he *could* give her a little hope for the future. That was all he'd been trying to do. It just…hadn't come out quite right.

What did he think he was saying? Had he really been promising her that she would meet someone and fall in love like Reece and Danielle? Honestly, that didn't happen for everyone, even people who weren't already living in a nightmare. In her case—he had no business making promises.

Ben slowly exhaled as he turned onto the highway and, sensing her watching him, glanced her way. The look on her face was a mixture of hurt and surprise that he felt—achingly—all the way to his bones.

They drove in silence through Salt Lake as Ben focused on maneuvering the highway and making sure they were not being followed. He hoped his chief had learned something from the man they'd captured. But with the way things were going, he couldn't quite manage optimism. Depending on how the events unfolded, the man could already be walking free.

The guy could be free to follow them again.

Or even if he stayed in police custody, someone new might be after them. If he wasn't working alone, which was highly likely, the next goon could have taken up his task.

Ben wished he could get Chasey to a safe house to wait while they worked toward finding the culprit behind it all, but they needed to get to Brighton. He glanced at Chasey again. She appeared lost in thought, staring out the passenger window.

"Hey," he said.

She turned to him, giving him a tenuous smile.

"Are you okay?" He shook his head at his own stupidity. "I keep asking you that stupid question."

She laughed. "It's not stupid, Ben. And… I'm okay. I mean… I'm going to be. It's like you said, eventually things will settle down. And next time, when I'm building a new life with a new identity, Brighton will be with me. I'm glad we're finally on our way. Only a few more hours."

"You're right. We should be there late tonight, as long as the weather doesn't delay us."

At the moment, there was no snow, but he knew that could change. Still, he wasn't about to take the route through the mountains on their way to Denver. Instead he would travel up through Wyoming and then down. The weather could be brutal, especially the wind, but at least it would be better than the mountains.

"Do you think we should call? It'll be too late to see Brighton once we get there. But if we call to let them know we're coming, maybe they'll give us some leeway on the usual visiting hours."

"No. I've been thinking about this. We don't want them to know we're coming. We don't want anyone to know our destination."

"Maybe we could just call to check in on him. I'd love to hear his voice to make sure he's okay. I didn't call him nearly enough. I tried to let him grow close to those at Holly House and not depend on me so much, for his own safety. What was I thinking?"

She glanced out the window but not before Ben saw the tears.

Ben knew she missed her brother, but he figured that on top of those feelings, seeing Reece and Danielle, coupled with Ben's own ridiculous words, had amplified Chasey's regrets, and her need for her brother, who was the only constant in her life.

Ben found his cell.

"Are you calling Brighton?" she asked.

"I'm calling my chief. I think I should get the latest update so I can make informed decisions." Like whether they should go through Wyoming or take another route.

His supervisor answered quickly. "Bradley, I have news. The man who followed you is named Milo Cash. He has no priors. He was previously a consultant for medical software, but is down on his luck and now driving for Uber. He claimed he was driving around the parking lot of the shopping mall, waiting for his girlfriend to get off work."

As the chief spoke, anger built in Ben's chest. "And you checked the girlfriend."

"Yes and no. A woman came by the police station to answer questions, claiming she was his girlfriend and that she worked for a candle shop."

"Claimed? What are you saying?"

"I'm saying she was questioned and let go before an investigating officer actually followed up on that and learned that the girlfriend did not work at the shop. In fact, I think she was paid to show up and support his cover story."

"So he's definitely not working alone—and he was hired by someone with enough resources to put plenty of people on this task."

"That's what we're thinking. But who is he really?"

"Are you thinking his background has been doctored?"

"It's hard to say, but no matter his background, he's somehow involved. This is going to our Criminal Intelligence Branch. They'll work with the locals to investigate as needed."

Too bad they hadn't been brought in from the start. Intellectually, Ben understood every agency had its processes, and sometimes people or incidents fell through the cracks between coordinating efforts, hence why CIB was only being brought in now. But understanding this did nothing to moderate his mounting frustration.

"Ben—" not "Bradley," per usual "—I need to ask. When will you have her somewhere safe? I'm concerned that you were discovered in Salt Lake. How were you tracked?"

"I think we've been followed all along, but I wasn't able to spot them. I strongly believe the man at the gas station wasn't actually there to commit a simple robbery. He's part of this, too. Someone else hired by our mastermind with deep pockets. He could have put a tracker on the Suburban, though I didn't see one. Any news on him?"

"He's not talking, and just made bail this morning."

Great. "He could skip bail."

"He could. Tell me how I can help."

"You know how—find who's behind this." And the sooner, the better.

"Call me tonight on my secure line." Chief Calvin spouted off the number. "I want to be able to call you if I need you."

"Will do." He ended the call. Ben hadn't shared the burner cell number because, under the circumstances, it was simply too risky. But no matter his over-the-top efforts, someone had still tailed them. As he looked in the rearview mirror, he feared they were still shadowing them.

To kill Chasey? To take her?

If killing her had been on the agenda then why hadn't the gas station burglar simply shot her instead of stuffing her in the trunk of his car? For that matter, the man on the lake could have shot her, also. Yes, he'd held a gun to her head to threaten her when Ben had approached, but prior to that, he could have taken her out easily enough if that was what he'd been after.

He grabbed her hand, gripping it tightly. He never wanted to let go. And yet, when this was over, he would have to let her go.

He focused his thoughts back onto the road. Knowing they could still be followed didn't change the route he had to take. The mountains would take longer and would be riskier.

As it was, they had about two hours before it would get dark and, with each passing mile, he had the sense that they weren't alone.

Whether he could spot someone tailing them or not, it was clear that somebody knew how to track them down. He had to face that truth and let it rip through him. And the truth was that Ben wasn't sure he could actually get Chasey somewhere safe, especially when he added her brother to the mix.

The reassurances and promises he'd made to her earlier were out of her reach.

They were out of his reach, too.

The highway through Wyoming arched across the lower half of the state. Chasey let her mind wander as she watched the peculiar landscape. While it was barren in some places, it was mostly beautiful and mesmerizing. Where she'd lived in California was gorgeous, especially after living in New York City surrounded by skyscrapers and mass population for so much of her life. Living in Manhattan was like living on an island of concrete and endless noise—from tourists, jackhammers, taxis, pedestrians, food cart vendors and dozens of other things. It was exhilarating and exciting, but quiet and peaceful it was not.

To her, these wide-open spaces were far more fascinating. The landscape seemed to go on forever without a building or hint of civilization—other than the highway, of course.

She tried to let the scenery calm her mind, but continued to glance at the side-view mirror to see if she could spot someone following them. But they couldn't be suspicious of every vehicle traveling in the same direction along the miles and miles of open road.

They'd stopped at a diner to stretch their legs and for a quick meal, but all Chasey had wanted was to rush through it so she could get to Brighton as soon as possible. Still, Ben had been right. They'd needed a decent meal and to take a break from driving.

Day had turned to night after dinner and she spent the time watching the night sky.

She never knew the stars could be so brilliant. She couldn't seem to stop looking at them. Maybe she would ask Ben to give her and Brighton new identities somewhere like Wyoming, away from all the light pollution, so she could become a stargazer. Yeah, Brighton would probably like that, too.

Chasey wasn't sure when it happened. Either they had caught up to a storm or one had moved in behind them, but the stars began to fade away, blocked by cloud cover as the night became truly black. She was struck by how genuinely dark it could be in the middle of a stretch of landscape without cities or towns for miles to reflect their light against the clouds.

She felt the vehicle shudder and glanced at Ben. He was gripping the steering wheel tightly. A light, drizzling rain started and a few moments later turned to snow.

It was tricky enough to drive in darkness for hours on end. Driving on slick roads, with not enough lighting…it was a daunting prospect. She'd enjoyed a few moments of calming reflection but now the tension ramped back up into her neck and shoulders. She gripped the handsets in the small sedan—small compared to the Suburban—as they followed a few car lengths behind an eighteen-wheeler moving too slowly.

She had the feeling Ben hesitated passing the truck as it weaved back and forth, its large frame shuddering and moving in the wind.

"Do you think he'll pull over at one of those truck stops?" she asked.

Ben smiled—for her benefit, she knew—but kept his eyes focused on the road. Even with the smile, his expression was somber. "I hope so, but on the other hand, he's leading the way on a dark and stormy night. I know it sounds weird, but it's almost kind of comforting."

No sooner had Ben said the words than the red trailer lights in front of them shifted one way then jerked severely the other direction.

"Oh no!" Chasey gasped. She squeezed the armrests. "He's fishtailing."

The sound of tires skidding across the pavement resounded through the confines of their car. Ben slowed the vehicle, putting distance between them and the out-of-control truck.

Lord, please help the driver keep that truck on the road.

The fishtailing grew wider and deeper.

Ben huffed next to her. "I don't like this."

The trailer evened out as the driver got control on the road. A slow breath eased from her lungs. "It's all right now, though, isn't it?" she asked.

"I wasn't talking about the truck," Ben said.

She glanced in her mirror to see fast-approaching headlights coming up behind them. "What do you think is happening?"

Even as she asked the question, she realized she already knew the answer—no one would be driving that fast on this road in this weather without a very good reason. Make that a bad reason.

"I'm not sure," Ben said, "but I'm going to pass the truck now or we'll be trapped behind him."

A sudden gale-force wind whipped snow around them, blinding them. It felt like the vehicle was sliding. Hands gripping the seat, Chasey bit back a scream. *Oh, Lord, I can't take this!*

She wanted to squeeze her eyes shut but then again, she needed to see the events as they unfolded. Ben moved into the left lane to pass the truck as the vehicle behind them sped up. It was a Suburban—a much bigger vehicle and a match for the one they had been driving before they had switched it out for a smaller rental sedan. Chasey spared a moment to miss the Suburban they'd left behind in the mall parking lot. It might have done a better job of protecting them now that their lives were, once again, at risk.

Yes, she had to admit that Ben was putting his life on the line for her.

He accelerated as he passed the truck, which seemed to slide closer to them as they slowly inched forward.

The headlights grew brighter from behind. "Ben..." She wished she could pull the word back. He didn't need any distractions or a passenger-seat driver.

"Hold on." Ben accelerated and passed the eighteen-wheeler.

Once he was past, the big truck suddenly slid into the middle of the interstate highway, essentially cutting off the vehicle closing in on them.

Was it too much to hope for that they could lose their follower? Was it the same guy who had found their Suburban in Salt Lake City, and whom the police had released earlier? Or someone new? Someone different?

The last glimpse Chasey had of the SUV was of the vehicle whipping onto the shoulder to avoid the rig. The trucker continued to struggle to control his massive vehicle on the slippery road and it slowed to a crawl. In her opinion, he should have slowed a long time ago.

Headlights whipped around the eighteen-wheeler as it finally moved back into the right lane. The speedy Suburban was gaining on them.

"Ben?" she whispered again, in spite of herself.

"I see it. Hold on and pray."

Oh well, she had never stopped praying, so that was an easy instruction to follow, even if forming coherent words was a little beyond her right now. Chasey closed her eyes and tried. The only word she could get out was *God*. She could only think to call out to God.

Lord!

She felt the sudden jolt as the Suburban bumped their car, sending it fishtailing into a full-on spin across the highway. Terror flooded her body. The sedan left the road, bouncing and cascading into the snow-filled ditch.

NINE

Heart thundering, pounding in his throat, Ben couldn't take the time to get his bearings. He had to act. Now.

But first things first. With a slow exhale, he twisted in his seat to look Chasey over, swallowing back his fear that she'd been hurt. "Are you all right?"

Her features were tight but when she turned to him, she appeared to shake off her shock. "Yes. I mean, I'm not injured, but no, I'm not all right. I'm scared."

Understandable. Time to get into gear. "I need you to put on your coat and get out of the car, then come around to my side of the vehicle but stand back and out of the way."

"What? Why?"

Because… "They're turning around." The Suburban, after veering onto the shoulder, had turned around. It was now making its way along the edge of the center median that separated the east-and westbound lanes of the interstate highway. "They're coming back for us."

To finish what they started.

Chasey reached into the back seat to grab the jacket she'd tossed there. She glanced at him and nodded, then scrambled out as Ben did the same. He watched the approaching SUV as Chasey shuffled around the front of the sedan to him.

He gestured into the darkness behind him. "Run, get back from the car, out of sight."

"What are you doing?" She gasped out the question.

"I'm going to end this. But I need you safely away. If things go wrong, then you're going to be on your own. I don't want him to catch you—I don't even want him to see you." Ben handed her the burner cell. "If that happens, the chief's number is in there and you need to call him."

He hoped things didn't go wrong, but at least she could make contact and get help. That was, if Ben failed her.

"You're scaring me." Chasey visibly shivered as the wind buffeted both of them. "Just come with me."

He struggled to resist the plea in her voice.

"This guy isn't going to stop. I need to give us the advantage. Now hurry. Time is running out." Without another word, Ben took off around the sedan Danielle had rented for them, heading toward the vehicle and driver threatening them.

The large SUV angled toward him as he stood ten yards from their sedan. The timing was right. No vehicles traveled on the highways in either direction at the moment. Ben aimed his Glock 9 mm and fired three shots. Windshield. Grill. Tires. The Suburban jerked to the side then, with the slippery conditions, rolled. Rocked a few seconds then rolled again, landing upside down. At least it remained in the wide median and hadn't ended up on the freeway.

Ben noticed that, up ahead, the eighteen-wheeler they'd passed had pulled to the side of the road. Clearly, the trucker had noticed what was going on. Was he calling the police? While police presence would give them a little protection, it would once again reveal their identities and locations. Why did everything always have to be a trade-off?

The man inside the Suburban was moving. He was trying to get out.

Ben hadn't shot him, had only meant to stop the vehicle. He wanted to get his hands on the driver so he could find some answers. Flipping on a flashlight he'd retrieved from the car to illuminate the area behind the Suburban's headlights, he pushed through the snow piling up and hiked over to the SUV. He would pull the guy out and question him while they waited for the police and possibly an ambulance to arrive.

"Ben!" Chasey called from behind. "Your cell phone is ringing. Should I answer?"

"No. Stay back. Go back to the sedan and get inside." He glanced over his shoulder then back to the Suburban.

The driver had successfully climbed out. Ben braced himself for the man to shoot, but instead he took one long look at Ben then suddenly turned and ran.

Are you kidding me?

Given his aggressive behavior on the road, Ben hadn't expected the guy to run. The most likely reason: he hadn't been able to reach or to find his weapon after the vehicle had flipped. Without it to defend himself, he hadn't wanted to fall into Ben's hands.

"Hey! Stop right there!" Ben aimed his Glock, hoping it would be enough of a deterrent. But he wouldn't shoot the man in the back—which the man must have guessed, because he kept running without even looking back. Ben started off after him.

A car honked and swerved, nearly landing in the ditch as the man jogged across the highway.

Just where did the guy think he was going?

A look over his shoulder confirmed that Chasey had gotten into the sedan to keep warm. Ben waited for a few cars to pass—and fortunately with the weather turning bad and the lateness, it wasn't too bad. He jogged across the two-lane highway and shone his flashlight in search of the man. There. About fifteen yards ahead. The guy was limping but still trying to run.

Almost got him. Almost there.

The man glanced over his shoulder as Ben shoved into him, knocking him to the snowy ground.

Ben grabbed his collar and took a good look at his face. It was the guy from Salt Lake City. Why hadn't the police held on to him to find out more?

"Who are you working for?" Ben demanded. "Who's behind this?"

The guy took a swing and Ben dodged the gloved fist but lost his hold on the man's collar. He reached for him again and they tussled and rolled. Ben had tucked his gun away in his holster. He needed the man alive.

But the guy produced a knife and slashed at Ben, cutting through his jacket. The man pressed the knife against Ben's throat. "I just want the woman. Tell me, is she worth your life?"

Was he about to die? Was this guy about to slice into his throat? Even if he was, Ben knew his answer.

"Absolutely." He then grabbed the attacker's wrist, disarming him, and reversed their positions to press him down into the snow. "Now it's your turn to talk. Just tell me who's behind this."

"I can't." The man slung a fisted arm around.

Ben blocked it, but the fist held a rock, which the man released. It slammed into Ben's head and he stumbled.

Blackness edged his vision, and he dropped to his hands and knees.

Must. Get. Up.

He remained on all fours, snow up to his thighs and growing. Unconsciousness beckoned, but he forced himself to push it away. If he didn't get up, Chasey could be in danger.

"Ben." Her soft voice spoke in his head. In his mind. She couldn't be here. She was in the car. He had to make it back to the sedan.

Where were the police?

"Ben." He felt her arms around his torso, trying to pull him upright.

He wasn't seeing or hearing things. She was really there. "You shouldn't be here," he said.

"Let's get you back to the car. He's gone.

The guy is gone. Come on, Ben. You're going to freeze out here."

He was supposed to be protecting her and here she'd come to find and save him. He scrambled to his feet. She shone a flashlight in his face and the bright light sent pain through his head.

"You're bleeding! Oh, Ben, did he stab you? Are you okay?"

"I'm fine. I'll be fine. Let's go."

He spotted the eighteen-wheeler still sitting there. The trucker got out as they started to cross the road. "Hey, man. I called the cops, but they said that with the roads like this, it might take a while before they can get here. Are you okay? You need the hospital or something?"

Ben eyed the sedan stuck in the snow. He'd need to call for a tow probably. And once the cops got here, that vehicle would be on someone's radar. But then, it was already on the bad guy's radar, wasn't it? After all, they'd clearly been found yet again. That meant they couldn't stay with the car, even if it was still drivable.

Ben glanced up at the trucker. "How far are you going?"

Chasey waited alone in the cab of the semi as Ben and Rolf, the trucker, spoke with the Wyoming Highway Patrol—outside in the wind and the cold. She assumed Ben had refused delaying them further by moving the conversation to the highway patrol's offices where it was warm and dry.

Glancing at her watch, she thought about this new delay. They would be in Denver already had they not been sidetracked by this latest attack—a man who was still on the loose, fleeing into this cold night. She assumed the local sheriff's department would be out there searching, maybe knocking on doors at rural houses to warn people and to find the man.

A tow truck was loading Danielle's rental car. She wondered how Ben had pulled that off without leaving a paper or digital trail. But maybe his chief was taking care of it all—Ben's boss had his back.

He also seemed to be the only one at the marshals' office who Ben was willing to trust. Given the fact that their attackers kept finding them, she might have questioned that trust, wondering if the man was the one exposing Ben's witnesses, but she trusted Ben's instincts. And anyway, if his chief were behind this, Chasey would likely already be dead or in the hands of her pursuers.

Shaking off her circling thoughts, Chasey decided to use the time to search for a way to make this seat more comfortable. She had their bags of clothes in her lap. The cab extended to create a tiny apartment with a table and seating that converted to a bed. It was like a small camper attached to the driver's cab, really. Since the front seats were captain's chairs instead of a bench seat for three, either she or Ben would have to sit in the back. She would have felt somewhat uncomfortable about that, but noticed a Bible on the table and a small cross dangling from a knob on the dashboard.

In the rearview mirror, she spotted Ben and Rolf heading back to the truck. Chasey slid out of the front seat and moved into the camper part of the cab with their meager belongings. Rolf opened the door, letting cold wind and snow rush in, as he climbed up into the driver's seat, his expression serious. That worried her.

He shifted around to spot her in the back and offered her a smile. "Please make yourself comfortable—I don't mind if you move things around."

Ben opened the passenger's-side door and climbed up into the cab. "You want to sit up here, Chasey? It's up to you."

"No, I'm fine. There's a table with a Bible." And with that, she slid into the seat and got herself settled. She wanted to talk to Ben and find out more about what had been said to the cops, what was going on, but she didn't feel free talking in front of Rolf.

Still… "Thank you for this, Rolf. For helping us get to our destination."

"Always happy to help." He started up the big rig and it rumbled to life. He slowly steered back onto the highway. "My sister was killed in a terrible accident."

Chasey wasn't sure why he had brought that up, but she would wait to see what more he said.

"I'm so sorry to hear that," Ben said.

"She would have survived if someone had been around to help her. She lost control of her car on a cold winter night, just like this, and ran off the road. She must have been knocked unconscious, because she was found behind the wheel, exactly where she would have been after the crash. She froze to death. If someone had just been there to check on her and called for help, she could have lived."

Tears surged in Chasey's eyes. This poor, dear man. "Oh, Rolf, I'm sorry for your loss. How long ago did it happen?"

"It's been five years. After that, I told the Lord I would always be available to help if I saw someone in need."

Okay. Now she got it. "That's why you waited on the shoulder to see how things unfolded when you saw that we'd been attacked."

He nodded. “It was pretty obvious there was some bad business going on when that car chased you down and ran you off the road. I wish I could have done more to stop it from happening at all.”

“Believe me, Rolf,” Ben said, “your assistance has been invaluable.”

“I couldn’t help but overhear you telling the highway patrol you’re a US marshal. I won’t ask questions. Don’t need to know. All I know is that you’re traveling with precious cargo.”

Chasey. The man was referring to Chasey.

“More precious than you know,” Ben said.

The way he said the words seemed to carry a deeper meaning behind them.

More precious than you know...

Chasey let those words curl around her heart. She puffed up a pillow, grabbed a folded fleece blanket and made herself comfortable on the small sofa.

“I’ll take you all the way to where you need to go. I’ll help in any way that I can,” Rolf said.

After that, the conversation shifted to hot rods, and it sounded like both Ben and Rolf were motor heads. Chasey’s lids grew heavy. She couldn’t imagine a safer place at the moment as she felt the peace that exuded from Rolf and his mission in life—to help those in need—wrap around her.

Rolf and Ben also had that in common…

"Chasey?" Hands gently shook her shoulders. "Chasey, wake up."

She blinked her lids open to see Ben staring down at her. His green eyes were filled with concern, along with another emotion she couldn't pin down. "Ben… Where?" She sat up, suddenly remembering. "I can't believe I fell asleep."

His cheeks hitched up and those dimples emerged. "We're here."

Chasey stood in the small cab space and realized that put her much too close to Ben. Stepping back, she folded the blanket and set it on the sofa. "In Denver?"

"We're across the street from a hotel near Holly House. Rolf parked his rig at a gas station. We'll need to walk the rest of the way, but it's not far."

Chasey and Ben grabbed their sacks.

"I feel like a hobo," she said. "Carrying my stuff in plastic sacks and hitching rides from truckers."

Ben assisted her down the semi's steps onto the snow-covered, slippery pavement. Chasey pulled on her coat, which felt much too thin at the moment. Her teeth chattered, though she thought it stemmed from nerves, excitement and a measure of fear to be so close to Brighton rather than being because of the cold.

"I'll carry our things." Ben reached for the bags and she let him. He gestured across the street. "I called in a reservation. Or rather, Rolf did."

"He did?"

"Yes. He got us a room."

Chasey thrust her hands in her pockets. "Where's Rolf? I want to thank him before we go to the hotel."

"He's getting the room key and will be right back."

She studied Ben and searched his intense gaze. "You told him?"

He slowly nodded. "Sometimes you have to trust others. You have to recognize when God has sent you help you didn't even know you needed."

She smiled at that. "Rolf is definitely a Godsend."

"We did the best we could to get here, despite the obstacles. As far as I know, no one has tracked us this far."

Unless someone already knows where Brighton is and is waiting for us here. But she feared saying those words out loud, as if putting them out there would give them weight and make them true. Instead, she changed the subject. "I take it Rolf will only be getting one room, because that would look suspicious otherwise."

Ben shrugged. "I didn't ask, but if he only gets one room, you don't have to worry. I'll sleep on the floor, if I sleep at all. My plan is to make a few calls and to work with you to get Brighton out."

"And then what?" They had struggled to even get here. What would it be like to attempt to stay incognito while traveling with her severely autistic brother?

Oh, Lord, help us.

"I'm working on it. I'll figure it out before we spring Brighton, don't worry."

Ben had meant for his words to reassure her, but she hadn't missed the uncertainty in his tone. The look in his eyes told her that he was carrying a heavy burden.

Ben was worried and that terrified her.

TEN

Spring Brighton?

What was he saying? While he knew Chasey wanted her brother to be with them, he still wasn't convinced that it was a good idea.

God, help me find the right way forward.

He spotted Rolf crossing the street. He was putting a lot of trust in Rolf, who was more or less a stranger, but Ben didn't doubt the guy had a good heart. Ben still believed that God had sent help right when he and Chasey had needed it.

The wind kicked up and an arctic gust blasted the both of them.

"Come on." He urged Chasey away from the semi and closer to the gas station/convenience store where the building could provide a little shelter from the wind and blowing snow.

Rolf jogged the rest of the way and joined them, puffing out white clouds into the night. "Sorry it took me so long." He handed them a couple of key cards. "You're in room number 212."

"Thanks, man," Ben said. "This isn't the usual way I do things. I'm not even sure I should—"

Rolf held up his hand. "You don't need to explain. Besides, I offered to help. You think you're compromised, and I have no doubt God put me in the right place at the right time to help you."

Chasey reached over and placed her hand on Rolf's coat sleeve. "I can't thank you enough. Is there anything I can do to repay you for your kindness?"

"Sure." Rolf grinned. "Get somewhere safe and live a good life. I'll be praying for you. Now, you'd better get out of the cold." His smile faltered.

Ben figured he was probably thinking back to his sister's untimely death. Rolf's comment was Ben's cue to usher Chasey into the hotel to a safe, warm room, complements of Rolf.

Ben nodded. "Thanks. We'll be in touch."

He wrapped his free hand around Chasey's waist and ushered her forward.

A glance at the west and the sky looked to be clearing, but he couldn't know how long it would stay that way. At the hotel parking lot, they hurried between the parked cars to a door at the back. Using the key card, he ushered her through the door so they wouldn't be spotted at the front desk. The fewer people who saw them, the fewer people who could identify them if anyone came around asking questions. No need to create more witnesses on this journey to a safe place.

Together they headed up the stairwell instead of using the elevator, and on the second floor moved quietly down the hallway. He noted the exits and counted the doors as they searched for their room. He was grateful for Rolf's generosity. He wasn't certain what his chief would think about him relying so much on a civilian but, considering the mastermind behind this had proved to be someone with deep pockets and a partner on the inside who was willing to go to extensive lengths to find them, Ben felt he needed all the help he could get. If they could only figure out who was helping the criminal from within the US marshals' offices, that would quickly change how Ben operated.

They reached their room. Ben handed off his sacks and opened the door and cleared the room before allowing Chasey all the way in. It was small, so a quick clear was enough to ensure that the room, closet, bathroom and shower were free of intruders or threats.

Once inside, he closed, locked and bolted the

door while Chasey tossed their bags on one of the two queen-size beds.

"Why don't you get some rest until the next step?" he said.

"I slept in the truck. You're the one who should sleep. There are two beds, so you don't need to sleep on the floor."

He eyed them, knowing he probably wouldn't fall asleep. "You go ahead. I need to make some calls. I'll make those in the bathroom and try not to disturb you."

"You really need some rest. I'm worried about you, Ben." Chasey shrugged out of her coat and rubbed her arms.

He couldn't think what to say in response, and instead just stared at her hazel eyes. She was so beautiful. She looked different from the woman he'd first met—now she was a redhead instead of a brunette—and she was just as striking. Just as lovely. She'd drawn his attention that first day when he'd been assigned to protect her while she'd waited for trial. Ben lived in a family of heroes—his older siblings and his parents—and he'd worked hard to live up to the family legacy. Doing his job and doing it right was important to him. He hadn't meant to fall for her—a witness he was protecting—but he hadn't been able to help himself.

He knew he'd hurt her before. He'd hurt

himself, too. A lump grew in his throat. Leaving her again after this was going to hurt even worse. But what other choice did he have? It wasn't like he could just walk away—any more than he could just stop loving her.

She shrugged, hurt flashing in her eyes at his lack of response. "Okay, well, please get some rest after you make your calls. I doubt I can sleep much, but you're right that I need to be prepared for what comes next, and for me that's seeing Brighton."

Chasey took a step toward him. "We *are* getting Brighton out, aren't we? Bringing him with us?"

And now came the hard part. He couldn't answer her questions because he was still trying to figure that out.

Lord, help me to know what's best for Brighton.

He took her hands in his and led her to the table, gesturing for her to sit while he took the other chair. "I brought you here, Chasey. You can look out the window and see the lights on Holly House. I know you needed this—needed to see him. As far as removing him from the facility where he's safe… I'm not sure if that's the best call. I thought I would have the answer by the time we got here, but there are still too many unanswered questions. I know you miss him, but moving him, taking him away from where he feels comfortable, would be traumatic for him—especially if we're going to have to spend more time on the run." Her brother was probably still adjusting, or maybe had only just now started feeling as if the place was home. How would he react to a situation as chaotic as theirs had been for the past couple days?

Tears welled in her eyes. "Of course I don't want to upset him or traumatize him—but I miss him. I no longer believe keeping us separated with different identities is for the best. I want us to get new identities and live together."

"Even if we do that, even if we resolve this current threat and I set you up living somewhere else, you know there's a risk that he will inadvertently give you away. And remember the whole reason you decided it was best that you live apart was that if the two of you weren't together, it would be more difficult for your uncle to track you—if he ever decided to do just that."

Chasey might not think that mattered right now, in the middle of these circumstances with her identity already discovered, but when she was settled into a new life, she'd once again have to live with the risk of it falling apart.

The tears sliding down her cheeks nearly ripped him up inside. He lifted a thumb and wiped the salty moisture from her cheek. He could tell she struggled to speak. Chasey was strong. She had to be to have endured so much and still find the courage to stand against her criminal uncle. But how much more could she take while still saying so gentle, so vulnerable inside?

How had she stayed so softhearted and tender?

Was it any wonder he'd fallen in love with her?

He took her hands in his again and spoke softly. "Let me think about it and talk to my boss. I promise, you get to make the final decision. But we want you to be fully informed before you make that choice. It's one thing to talk about *your* life, Chasey, but Brighton is depending on you."

Brighton was depending on them both.

Chasey slipped her hands free from Ben's strong, reassuring grip. She didn't like what he'd had to say, but she knew that she couldn't just ignore it. Not when he was only speaking out of a desire to keep her and her brother safe. She trusted him as much as anyone could be trusted. She was trusting him with her life. And as he'd said, Brighton was depending on her. So her trust in Ben included trusting him with Brighton's life, as well.

She nodded and looked away, and that seemed to satisfy Ben.

He got up and stared at the cell phone, flicking the lights off on his way to the bathroom. "Try to get some rest, okay?" He slipped into the bathroom and shut the door. The light bled from underneath it.

Chasey glanced at the fluffy pillows and inviting bed. She would get there eventually but first she moved to the window and peeked out into the cold night. Had they even gotten an actual autumn? It sure felt like winter was settling in early and with a vengeance.

A couple of blocks away, she spotted the roof of Holly House—it wasn't an actual house but more like a campus or compound of apartments that offered assisted living plus security. It was very secure, but also very isolated. In a way, she had sacrificed Brighton's freedom for his safety. Was it more important to be free or to be safe? That was a call she hadn't allowed Brighton to make for himself, which meant that the decision—like all other decisions about Brighton's care and what was best for him—rested on her shoulders. Any mistake she made could be disastrous, for both her and her brother.

Lord, why is any of this happening?

She considered how things might have

turned out differently if Brighton had been with her from the start. Would Ben have put her in the same region of the country, or in a different situation entirely? She still would have required help for Brighton, so perhaps she would have ended up in a more densely populated area with better public services to help him.

But she would still have been found. And if Brighton had been there when the attacker had come to her house, he could have been hurt or killed.

Ben was right—their next steps, the decisions she would make, could mean life or death for her brother. In addition, whatever move she made could have an impact on her future guardianship of Brighton. She sat on the edge of the bed, unable to sleep. Even though Ben was just in the bathroom, it still made her a little uneasy to have him a room away.

Chasey heard his voice in the bathroom, then silence, as if he was listening. Then a few more words. She wished she could eavesdrop on the conversation because, of course, it had to be about her and this situation.

She eyed the phone that rested on the desk. A regular, landline phone and not a cell. She could call Brighton. Her heart tripped inside, [illegible] as she reminded herself that it was approaching 4:00 a.m. While someone would answer the phone at the facility at any hour, she doubted they'd be willing to wake Brighton to make him come to the phone.

Chasey heard a car door shut in the parking lot outside the window and glanced out. Below she saw two men heading toward the back door; one of them clearly held a pistol in his hand.

The desk phone rang, startling her.

Ben stepped into the room, the bathroom light casting his shadow across the floor.

"Should we get it?" she asked.

He took two steps forward and picked up the receiver. She could clearly hear Rolf's voice on the other end, though she couldn't catch what he had to say.

"Thanks." Ben hung up and rushed to the window to peer out. "We've got trouble."

"What kind of trouble? Is it Brighton?"

"Someone found us."

"I saw two men entering the hotel just now. But how did they find us?"

"That was always a risk. The guy in the Suburban must have contacted whoever he worked for and told them about the semi." Ben pressed his hand against the gun in the holster he'd never taken off.

The room seemed to close in around her. She didn't know why now, but suddenly the sound of gunfire from the past accosted her, echoing around her as though it was happening here and now. Chasey covered her ears. She didn't want to hear more of it. She squeezed her eyes shut but that couldn't block the images from two years ago—her uncle shooting a man in his office in cold blood right before her eyes. She gasped for breath.

God, help me breathe!

Ben took her wrists and lowered her hands. She opened her eyes to peer at him.

"Come away from the window." He peered at her, concern in his gaze.

"I… I had a flashback."

"That happen often?"

"No, it's never happened before. I don't know why it happened now. I guess… I guess because we're so close to Brighton. The pressure and the fear are getting to me. They found us again. Where can we go? What can we do?" She slumped onto the bed. "I'm so tired of running."

He crouched in front of her. "And this is exactly the moment when it's most important that we not stop. Things usually get worse before they get better."

And then he smiled. Dimples cut into his cheeks. While she usually loved the sight, at this moment, it did nothing but frustrate her.

"How can you smile at a time like this?"

Oh, she wished she could pull the words back when the smile faded.

"I'm sorry. I was only trying encourage you. To take the edge off." He stood and moved away from her.

Chasey instantly felt the absence of his warmth.

Ben paced the room as if he struggled to know what they should do next, too, and that was never a good sign.

"The only way they can find us is to harass the guy at the front desk. He never laid eyes on us, but he can say which room was just rented out," he said. "Rolf is calling the police."

"But you don't want anyone, including the police, to know we're here."

"He isn't telling them about us. He is going to tell the police that he spotted two suspicious and armed characters entering the hotel."

"So…we wait here?"

"Maybe." Ben headed to the window and peered out again. "They're here."

"Who? The police?"

"Yes."

"So can we relax now that they're here?"

"No. I don't want us to be trapped here, either."

"Trapped?"

The fire alarm blared.

ELEVEN

The sound ricocheted through Ben. It was definitely not what he wanted to hear. He held Chasey's gaze and recognized the fear ramping up.

"The fire alarm?" It was a question. Her tone was incredulous.

"They must be trying to flush us out," he said.

"So is there a fire or not?" She started pacing the small room and her breaths quickened.

"Calm down." *While I think.*

"Do not tell me to calm down, Ben. The fire alarm is blaring. We need to leave. We need to get out."

"There might not be a fire. Someone could have hit the alarm just as a pretext to get everyone out of their rooms." It seemed likely, given that two armed men had entered the hotel. Yes, they could have started a fire. But would they have had enough time? They'd only just arrived a minute earlier.

"What are we going to do?" She held her hands out, looking to him for answers.

He peered out the window and spotted more police cruisers steering into the parking lot, lights flashing. Pulling out his phone, he sent a quick text message to the chief, updating him on the situation.

Protecting Chasey—protecting his witness—was always his priority. The questions and doubts entered the equation when he had to figure out *how* to fulfill his mission under such circumstances. Doors in the hallway opened and closed. Voices echoed. All of the other guests were at least leaving their rooms, whether or not they were evacuating the building.

Should he rush Chasey out into that crowd and hope to get lost in it? Or should they wait in this hotel room on the theory that there wasn't truly a fire? If they waited and ended up being the last people to leave the hotel, they would more easily be spotted and potentially picked off. But waiting would mean that Chasey wasn't exposed to possible gunfire until the last possible second. And by that time, emergency workers—firemen and more cops—would provide a protective wall between Chasey and the people who wanted her captured or killed.

Once again, he glanced out the window that overlooked the side of the hotel. People were already rushing to their vehicles—some to get away from the chaos, others to simply keep warm. Which door could they exit if they needed to, and still be safe? Would their pursuers be watching the doors? Which ones?

Rolf had only seen two men enter the hotel, but that didn't mean more weren't waiting and watching from the parking lot or other locations.

"Ben?" Chasey's voice broke through his orbiting thoughts.

He turned to look at Chasey.

"I smell smoke," she said. "It's more than someone pulling the fire alarm."

His eyes weren't burning yet, but he knew the toxic gases in smoke could definitely kill them long before a fire. The men had taken things further than simply barging into the hotel to search for them, and setting the fire alarm off.

These men—now they had at least two if not more after Chasey—were more determined than ever to get to her. But setting a fire in a hotel? How many lives were these people willing to risk just to capture Chasey? A truck's honk drew Ben's attention to the window. Across the lot, parked in the street that ran next to the hotel, was Rolf's semi. The man had seen the chaos. He knew that Ben and Chasey needed a way out. Again.

Rolf was in effect putting himself in the line of fire.

Ben grabbed Chasey's hand, pulling her from the window toward the door. His gun ready to fire, he peaked through the peephole and saw nothing. Then he slowly opened the door.

Footsteps pounded down the hallway, along with the sounds of people knocking on doors and men announcing that the hotel was being evacuated. They turned a corner—two men dressed as firemen. Were they legit? Or had they incapacitated the real firemen? Ben's gut soured.

Two men carrying guns.

Nope. Not firemen at all.

Ben eased the door shut, putting the security latch in place. "Get over in the corner by the bed." He gestured where she should hide.

Chasey moved quickly. "We could go out the sliding-glass door to the balcony and climb over and hang down. It wouldn't be that far of a jump."

"Yes, it would. Even if we could do it without getting hurt, we'd be too exposed. There could be other men waiting for us down in the parking lot or on the street." He lifted his fingers to his lips.

The pounding on doors and voices grew louder as the men approached.

They were at the next room. So far, they hadn't kicked down any doors or shot any hotel guests, though they'd kept up the pretense of knocking on every door. Was that because they genuinely didn't know which room Ben and Chasey were in—or because they wanted them to let their guards down?

He backed away from the door and ducked against the wall, holding his gun at the ready.

He inhaled slowly, counted to four, then held his breath for another count of four.

Exhaled... *One, two, three.*

The pounding came at their door. Ben would keep quiet. Maybe they really didn't know what room the two of them were in. Even if they knew, Ben had bolted the door.

The telltale click sounded and the door partially opened before the security latch stopped it.

Ah. Now they knew that someone was inside the room. But did they know it was Ben and Chasey?

"Please evacuate. There's a fire in the hotel."

Ben braced himself for what would come next.

Hotels had a tool for unlocking the security latch in case someone was unconscious or unable to reach the door for some reason—such as an untimely death. And, of course, there was always the possibility that they'd kick in the door, breaking the latch. If the men were determined to get in, they'd find a way. He glanced back at Chasey, and her big eyes stared at him.

Fear poured from her gaze as she slowly nodded, but he saw something more behind that look. She trusted him. They were in this together. She had no idea how much that trust, that confidence in his ability—no matter if it was misplaced—bolstered his resolve.

This was his job. He didn't have time for the many doubts that had accosted him. In this moment, he just had to trust his training and act.

The door burst open.

Chasey failed to stifle her scream. But she successfully resisted the physiological reflex to squeeze her eyes shut and wait for the danger to pass.

From the corner where she was crouched, she saw a gun slide into view, connected to an outstretched arm. Ben immediately disarmed the man, and landed several punches. Gunshots erupted from out in the hallway.

Ben stood still and stared out.

Oh no! Had he been shot?

No, his shoulders relaxed and he turned to face her. "Wait here."

"What's going on? Ben?" She rose and stepped to peer out from behind the open door.

Ben stood in the hallway, speaking to a police officer. He revealed his credentials. The "fireman" was being handcuffed.

Ben came back into their room and stood over the other unconscious "fireman." Then he moved to stand next to her between the bed and the wall as another officer entered the small space. The new arrival rolled the man posing as a fireman onto his stomach as he started waking up, cuffed him, then pulled him to his feet.

"Wait here," the officer said. "Someone will be in to get your statement."

"What about the fire?" she asked, glancing between the officer and Ben.

"The fire was small and has been put out. There's no need to evacuate, and you're safer in here, it would seem." The officer eyed Ben as if he understood Ben was protecting a witness. "We got a call about these guys, and someone from your agency's CIB will be questioning them."

Ben tensed and then his shoulders relaxed as though relief had whooshed through him.

She didn't know what CIB was, but at least someone would question these men. Hopefully, they would finally get some answers.

She knew Ben hadn't wanted to reveal their identities even to the police, but with the constant barrage of bad guys closing in on them, it was hard to avoid contact with law enforcement.

Besides, attempting to keep a low profile hadn't done much to hide them from their pursuers. Whoever was after her was closing in.

Tonight was another close call.

She didn't have to wonder who was behind this.

It was her uncle, of course. She'd been afraid of him for as long as she could remember. A year ago, when she'd testified against him and seen him convicted and sent to jail, she'd thought the fear could finally end, that she could move on with her life.

And a year later—look at her now.

The officer ushered the fake fireman out into the hallway. "Close your door and lock it. It'll keep the smoke out, as well. We'll send someone up to take your statement soon."

"Will do." Ben bolted the door. He wet a towel in the bathroom and stuck it to fill the crack under the door. "That'll keep the remaining smoke out."

"Do you trust that officer?"

"I didn't get a bad sense off him, so I don't think he's an immediate threat to us, no. But I didn't tell him we would stay, either."

"We're not going to give our statements?"

"We're going to figure out our next steps," Ben said firmly. "And if the best option is to leave immediately, then that's what we'll do."

Chasey glanced out the window. "Rolf is still waiting out there. Maybe we should—"

Ben glanced up from his cell phone. "You felt safe with him, didn't you?"

Was that hurt in his eyes? "No, Ben. I feel safe with you. But you have to admit, nothing happened to us while we were in his truck."

Ben tucked his cell away and approached her next to the window. What was he doing? He hung his head and sighed. She'd never seen him look so defeated.

He lifted his forest green eyes to her. "I'm sorry, Chasey. I feel like I've let you down. I—"

"Shh. Please, don't." She pressed her hand against his mouth. Oh, now why had she done that? Touching his lips sent tingles all the way through to her toes.

And Ben…

He kissed her palm where it was pressed

against his lips. She should pull her hand back but she couldn't move. He lifted his hands to her cheeks and cupped her face. Then he inched closer, lingering millimeters from her lips. Her pulse pounded in her ears as she waited for the kiss.

Oh please, kiss me. She closed her eyes, waiting, anticipating…and then she felt his mouth against hers. His lips were gentle but strong against hers where he lingered. The stubble on his face was rough and prickling, but she relished it all the same.

"Ben…" She whispered his name against his mouth.

Ben ended the kiss—filled with so much emotion that her head, her heart, was spinning—and pressed his forehead against hers. "If anything happened to you, I don't know what I would do. I… I'll protect you with my life. You know that."

"I know."

I know. And the fear of Ben giving his life to save her wouldn't let her go.

"I don't want you to have to protect me if it comes to that." She stepped back, out of his embrace. Out of his arms where she wanted to stay forever. "I never asked for any of this."

She rubbed her arms, feeling suddenly chilled.

"Ben, I need you to do more than protect me physically."

His brow furrowed. Hurt and regret filled his eyes as his lips turned downward. His Adam's apple bobbed. "I shouldn't have kissed you. I'm sorry."

Chasey stood taller and slowly inhaled. She was strong and refused to allow the overwhelming emotions she felt for this man—and that he, apparently, felt for her—overpower her. "You know what happens when this is all over. You go your way and I go mine."

Ben opened his mouth to say more—but just then someone knocked on the door.

He pulled his weapon out and she moved to her previous protective position between the bed and the wall.

Ben didn't move to open the door, nor did he ask who was knocking. Instead he waited and listened. It could be more of the same ilk that had tried to fake their way in as firemen.

Too many questions bombarded her. Just how many men were after her? Why now? Why had she not dealt with this degree of harassment back when she was set to testify against her uncle?

"It's Officer Farrow. I was here earlier."

Ben stepped up to the door, apparently recognizing the man's voice. Good enough for Chasey.

Officer Farrow entered the room and Ben explained about the fire and spotting the two men with guns heading down the hallway. More than that, he didn't say. He didn't offer up that she was running for her life or that this was just another in a string of attacks that they'd experienced over the past few days. Then Chasey shared the same story with the officer. As she answered his questions, she tried not to glance out the window, fearing that somehow he would know she was worried about her brother who lived in a facility two blocks over, even though she hadn't mentioned Brighton to the officer.

Officer Farrow closed his notepad. "You should know the hotel manager is talking about encouraging guests to find other accommodations as soon as possible, and offering a full refund. They plan to work on repairs from the fire as soon as possible."

"Thanks for the heads-up." Ben walked him to the door and shut it behind him, then bolted it again.

He remained at the door for a few moments, his head down. She wondered if, like her, he was thinking about the conversation they'd been having before the officer had interrupted. Chasey wanted to finish that conversation, even if she suspected she already knew what he would say—and that it would be something along the lines of how they could never be together.

Why were they going through this struggle again—the physical threat to her life and the emotional threat to her heart?

I don't understand, God.

"What now, Ben?" Her question to him was about their next move, whether they should stay here at the hotel or go somewhere else. But deep inside, she knew the question went much deeper, and she suspected Ben did, too.

"We'll be moving soon. But I need to finish my earlier conversation."

Her heart jumped. He would tell her what he would have said?

Except he lifted his cell phone to his ear. He hadn't meant his conversation with her, but his conversation with his supervisor, the one that had been interrupted when Rolf had called.

TWELVE

While Ben left a voice mail with his chief, he noticed Chasey cough a few times. The smoke still lingered in the air. They wouldn't stay here one minute longer than necessary. Already, guilt suffused him that he'd kept her here even this long.

She flicked her eyes at him before turning away. He, too, turned his back to her before she saw the tumultuous emotions in his eyes.

Anguish twisted in his gut.

God, why does my every move end with us back under the crosshairs?

What am I doing wrong?

One thing he was definitely doing wrong was leading Chasey on. Leading himself on. He wasn't doing it intentionally, but a man who had his act together would never have kissed her. He was embarrassed to admit to himself that when she'd pressed her hand against his lips, he had lost all control. He hadn't even realized how powerful the emotions were that he'd been keeping in check.

Her hazel eyes were like deep oceans filled with a formidable elixir he couldn't resist. The truth he hadn't wanted to admit was that he'd never gotten over her. He had to find a way to live with the weight of his hopeless love while he was with her. And then, on the other side of this, when, as she'd said, they went their separate ways.

Still…shame on him for kissing her.

Going down that road would only hurt them both, and Ben had never wanted to hurt her again.

He had a feeling that Chasey hadn't simply forgotten about him and moved on any more than he had. Not with the way she'd returned his kiss, the passion and emotion he'd felt just on the other side of that gentle connection.

It wasn't fair to stay on as her protector when he must be upsetting her just by being near her. If he could, he would give her security over to someone else, but how could he do that when he didn't trust anyone else to keep her safe?

But, Lord, help me to protect her. Help me get her to a safe place with a new identity. Chasey and Brighton both, if that's what she needs to be happy.

The sense of being watched—but not in a

bad way—drew him back to the moment. He suddenly realized she was watching him, and he hitched half a grin—for her sake. "Come on, let's get out of here."

They were the proverbial sitting ducks in this hotel room now, not to mention Chasey was still coughing.

"Where are we going? It seems like I've asked that question a hundred times."

"I'm not entirely sure," he said. "I'm making this up as I go. Can't you tell?" He made sure the hallway was safe before she joined him.

"I think mixing things up is probably the best plan. If you don't know what you're doing, then neither will the men after me." She almost looked like she was about to laugh.

He didn't linger to find out and instead led her to the exit at the end of the hall. Ben glanced back at her, and caught her beautiful grin. She was teasing him, and he could do no less than offer her a grin in return. Her eyes widened as she glanced from his mouth to his eyes. He pulled his gaze from her to focus on entering the stairwell. His gun, at the ready, led the way as she followed closely behind him.

She knew the drill well enough by now.

"The question is," she said, "just how many men are after me? Do you think the police will get something out of the two fake firemen?"

"I hope so. I also told Officer Farrow to contact the FBI."

"Do you think that more agencies knowing I was here will jeopardize our safety?"

"It's possible. That's why we need to move and fast."

"But what about Brighton?"

Ben held his hand up, signaling for her to wait for more conversation as they made their way to the exit to leave the building. He pushed the door slowly open. The frosty air hit him and he tucked his jacket tighter around him. He glanced around. Emergency vehicle lights still flashed from the parking lot. Other guests and hotel staff were still sitting in their parked cars.

Moving her like this was a risk. But staying was also a risk.

He heard the semi's diesel engine rumbling idle across the street. Rolf was watching and waiting. But Rolf could do no more for them. Someone would always follow them in the man's truck and continuing to accept Rolf's help would just put the trucker in more and more danger. Still, Ben would make his way to his new friend. They could at least regroup for a few moments—and thank him for his earlier warning call.

"Let's go." He grabbed Chasey's hand. Together they headed across the parking lot toward Rolf's truck.

Rolf opened up the cab of his truck and Chasey climbed in.

"Thanks, friend," Ben said. "I need to make a call and then I'll join you."

"I've got hot coffee waiting inside when you're ready."

Ben couldn't thank the man enough. He called his chief again and relayed all the information regarding the latest aggressive tactics. "This has to be her uncle behind this. What can we do to stop him? I need to get her somewhere safe and, right now, I'm struggling to lose the man after us. It shouldn't be so hard." Ben realized he was on the verge of yelling at his boss and forcibly calmed his words. His frustration was coming through. His lack of sleep and exhaustion were spilling out. "What have you learned?"

Ben bit back the barrage of a hundred more questions that he wanted to ask.

"I have some news, Ben."

"Well, what is it?"

"You're not going to like it."

Chasey held the stainless-steel thermal travel mug containing hot coffee in one hand and eased her other hand to the cab's door handle. She planned to give the coffee to Ben to keep him warm as he stood out in the cold. She opened the door and climbed down the steps. From the cab of Rolf's semi, she could see the hotel, still ringed with two firetrucks, several police cruisers and scores of emergency personnel. From what the officer had told them earlier while they were giving their statements, no one had been hurt aside from a little smoke inhalation. But it could have been so much worse.

Because of her.

The men after her had put so many lives in danger.

How was she supposed to deal with that?

Ben stood at the back of the eighteen-wheeler, white clouds from his breath puffing out as he spoke. The conversation sounded more like an argument. He shifted back and forth and his shoulders bunched up. His tone sounded tense, rose and then dropped suddenly as if he remembered where he was. He wouldn't like her eavesdropping, but this was her business, too.

Her life.

Brighton's life.

She advanced slowly, but even so, she expected him to hear her approach. It was part of his job to always be aware of his surroundings.

And before she was too close, he turned, shock and regret registering in his eyes.

It was too late.

She'd heard the words out of his mouth.

And dropped the thermal coffee mug. Hot coffee spilled out onto the frozen slush, steam rising.

"My uncle escaped prison?"

Ben grasped for her but she stepped out of his reach before he could connect. He continued his conversation, sounding like he was trying to end the call, but of course, with this new development, he had to stay on the line to get all the relevant information. Meanwhile, she backed toward the passenger door of the truck. Rolf leaned out of the passenger seat, looking between her and Ben.

Ben signaled for Rolf to help her.

Brighton. Oh, Brighton.

She knew what her uncle planned.

She *knew* her uncle was coming for Brighton. She didn't know how she knew, but she was still absolutely certain of it, down to her bones. She turned and approached Rolf, noting his concerned expression. Was he reading her, trying to anticipate her next moves? She had a feeling that if she tried to walk away, he would stop her, knowing that that was what Ben would want him to do. She wasn't a prisoner but had chosen to go into WITSEC.

And her next move would be her own decision, too. She dashed passed the opened door, around the front of the truck. Shouts erupted behind her, Ben and Rolf both. She didn't care what either of them wanted at the moment.

All her thoughts converged into one.

Brighton. She had to get to Brighton.

At the end of the day, at the end of this chaos, Brighton depended on one person only. Not Ben.

Brighton depended on Chasey, his guardian.

She might employ protection, or depend on other protectors, like Ben, but ultimately, Brighton's safety depended on the decisions she made.

And she was making a big one right now.

Crossing the street, she dashed down alleys, between stores and houses until she'd traveled the two blocks to the facility. Streetlights were at each corner of the complex, so there were no real shadows. She heard footfalls coming up behind her, but she was a runner and, even in this frozen landscape, the cold arctic air, she would beat them to the front door and spring Brighton from the virtual prison where she had placed him under the foolish idea that it would keep him hidden from their uncle.

God, forgive me for that mistake!

A sound drew her attention to the sky as she cut diagonally across the expansive snow-covered lawn toward the entrance.

Whop-whop-whop.

A helicopter? Chasey headed toward the walls of the building and out of the way of the helicopter. She had no idea who would be landing in the field. And she didn't care. Across the way, she spotted Rolf and Ben looking at her. They were too far back to catch up and they also backed off when the helicopter landed, skirting the edges of the lawn.

To her surprise, two men rushed from around the front of the building, dragging someone between them. Someone screaming.

That voice. That upset, hysterical voice reached her ears, sounding all too familiar. The men ushered the young man onto the helicopter and shut the door. Realization dawned much too slowly as she eyed the helicopter, which immediately lifted off the ground.

"Brighton!" Chasey ran toward the helicopter and waved her arms, jumping up and down as though she could stop the helicopter and save her brother through sheer force of will. *I'm here, Brighton. I'm here!* "Brighton. Oh, God, please help us!"

The helicopter hovered a moment. A face appeared in the window, illuminated by the lights around the facility. She'd hoped Brighton would look down and see her. But now…

Her uncle saluted her, then the helicopter rose higher and flew over the facility, disappearing into the predawn morning.

Chasey watched in shock, listened to the sound of the rotors growing distant.

Strong arms lifted her from the ground where she'd fallen in the snow.

"Stop it!" She struggled free and stepped away, anger flooding her soul. "My uncle took Brighton! He's gone, Ben, he's gone."

"Come here." Ben reached for her.

"No." Chasey stepped away from him. She didn't want to be consoled. She freely let the tears burn down her cheeks. "You let me down, Ben. You let this happen. I told you we had to get to Brighton. We could have gone straight here when we got to Denver instead of going to the stupid hotel."

Anguish filled her soul and she didn't know what to do with it.

She turned her back to Ben, but not before she caught the pain in his eyes. She'd been harsh on him, but she couldn't really bring herself to care. Her brother was in danger.

"He's going to use Brighton against me, don't you understand?"

"Yes, Chasey. I understand that I've let you down, but now we have to focus on saving Brighton. We're not doing him any good standing here. Let's get out of the cold."

He was right. She was letting her emotions get to her. There was no backtracking on the mistakes made. They had to move forward. She turned to face him and their new friend, Rolf. "Let's go inside to the facility. I want answers. No one should have released my brother without my authorization. I'm the guardian."

A couple of police cruisers pulled up to Holly House along with an FBI vehicle. Chasey flicked her gaze to Ben. "Did you—"

He shook his head. "Looks like he was taken forcibly and they have contacted the authorities."

"Let's go, then." She ran toward the front of the facility.

Ben grabbed her arm and whirled her around. "You're already in danger, Chasey. There's nothing you can do for your brother there. Let the authorities find out what happened. Come with me. We'll find someplace safe and then we can make a plan to find your brother."

She noted he stopped short of saying that he promised—either that they would find Brighton or that he would be unharmed. Her vision blurred as she walked between Ben and Rolf.

Footfalls approached from behind and Ben quickly turned, his weapon ready at his side.

"Rolf, please get her back to your truck."

An FBI special agent approached and Ben flashed his credentials.

Chasey rushed away with Rolf, leaving Ben to deal with the feds.

She thought back to Ben's earlier words, referring to Rolf. *You felt safe with him, didn't you?*

Those words had pierced her heart. Rolf was a man who believed God had put him in their path to help, but he was a man out of his depth. He just didn't know it yet.

No, Ben... I feel safe with you.

She still meant it, despite the horrible words she'd said to him just moments ago.

But the truth stared her in the face.

Ben couldn't protect her anymore. In fact, Ben would prevent Chasey from doing whatever she needed to do to save her brother.

Chasey was Brighton's only hope.

She just needed the right moment and, when it came, she would take action.

THIRTEEN

At the entrance to Holly House, Ben spoke with the feds and the local police about Chasey's abducted brother. It was a predicament no deputy US marshal, no WITSEC inspector, wanted to find himself in—when someone who needed protection and a new identity was taken from a secure location and put in harm's way. Finding and bringing them back to safety would require assistance many agencies.

In this situation, not knowing who could be trusted left Ben with a pounding headache and fear like he'd never known.

But he couldn't solve the issue with the leak in the department. All he could do was to look at the situation in front of him and try to find answers. How had Brighton's uncle been able to find him? Had it only been a matter of time, given the limited number of facilities that offered the type of care Brighton needed?

Either Brighton had been found because of

that or, as Ben feared, he and Chasey had led her uncle to Holly House and to Brighton. They had been followed for the entire time, despite their best efforts, and the next thing after they arrived—Brighton had been taken.

So yeah. Ben leaned more toward the young man's abduction falling on Ben. And once he'd been found, well…what happened next was a foregone conclusion. Places like Holly House weren't set up to face off with armed mercenaries. To protect the others, they had given up Brighton.

He fumed at this turn of events. *God...why? Just...why?*

Dragging a hand down his face, he tried to ignore the utter exhaustion clawing at him. He was at the end of his rope here, even before the abduction, and was grateful for Rolf's sudden appearance in their lives—a man he knew he could trust. Because right now, Ben couldn't face Chasey's heartbreak.

And in that way, he was letting her down. He should be able to carry this burden for her and with her. That was exactly what he'd do—in a minute, after he'd pulled himself together. He'd also use that minute to firm up his resolve and remind himself that he couldn't pull her into his arms to comfort her when she was vulnerable and needed him the most. Neither of them needed the additional heartbreak that growing closer was sure to bring.

Once he felt more settled, he pushed through the facility doors and stepped outside, leaving the locals to deal with the rest of gathering intelligence and evidence regarding Brighton's abduction. Time for Ben to face Chasey.

He walked around the block in the shadows, heading for the eighteen-wheeler near the hotel.

Lord, what do I tell Chasey?

Where do I even take her that's safe?

...Or does that even matter anymore?

Now that her brother was in his clutches, Chasey's uncle could very well use Brighton to lure Chasey to him. The best, most secure hiding spot wouldn't protect her if she'd turn herself over willingly to protect Brighton. Ben wasn't sure how the next few hours would play out. He had no idea what to expect.

As he neared the truck, Rolf stepped into view, the man's face twisted in agony. "I'm so sorry."

"It wasn't your fault that we didn't get to Brighton in time. You did all you could do to..." Wait. Rolf was referring to something entirely different. Ben sensed that in his bones. "What do you mean you're sorry. What's happened?" He rushed forward and looked inside the cab. "Where's Chasey?"

"She's gone."

Gone? Ben let the words sink in but found that he couldn't believe them. "What do you mean gone?" He stumbled forward and grabbed the man's collar. "Tell me, Rolf."

"We were set to climb into the cab and wait for you, but then she was just gone."

"Did you see her? Did someone take her?"

"I saw." He gestured to the far corner. "She got into a cab alone, all on her own free will. Her choice. I started to call your cell but I don't have that number."

Nobody had it—a senseless precaution that amounted to nothing.

Ben realized he still held Rolf's collar and released him. He scraped his cold bare hand through his hair and paced.

"I'm sorry," he said to Rolf. "I shouldn't have grabbed you like that—I know it's not your fault. Just...please tell me everything you remember. Every detail."

"On the way back to the truck, she cried a lot and mumbled about needing to find her brother. I thought she was beside herself and I didn't think she meant literally going to find him herself. I opened the door for her and she climbed in. I went around to my side and got in, too. She wasn't sitting up front, but I thought she was in the back like she had been before."

"And then what happened?"

"I spotted a cab pull up at the corner and Chasey got in. I started to get out to ask her what she was doing, where she was going, but I wasn't fast enough and the cab pulled away before I could reach it. I'm so sorry, man. I meant to help you."

"Did you get the cab number?"

"No, I didn't even think to look. I feel just awful. Like I've only made things worse."

Ben understood those sentiments. "You helped us make it through the night, Rolf. Don't doubt that you have helped us. But Chasey has her own mind and you couldn't stop her from making that decision. If anyone is to blame, it's me."

Rolf shook his head. "You need to take your own advice. You've helped her stay alive this long."

"But it wasn't enough. And now the person after her has her brother."

"What will he do with Brighton?" Rolf asked. "Will he hurt him?"

"I don't know. I think his primary purpose for taking him, though, is to use Brighton to get to Chasey. We were never sure if the people after her were trying to kill her or just trying to take her away, but now I think they were simply trying to abduct her all along."

“What can I do to help now?” Rolf asked.

Ben squeezed his shoulder. “Give me your card so my offices can compensate you for gas and time and the hotel.”

“Oh, there’s no need.”

“Yes, there’s need. And even if you think there isn’t, give me the card anyway. I’d like to stay in touch.”

Rolf handed Ben his card and he stuffed it in his pocket. “You have a load to deliver,” Ben said, “so I’ll let you get on your way. I’ll hitch a ride from the feds still at the facility.”

Rolf shook Ben’s hand. “God be with you.”

“You, too, Rolf. Say a prayer or two for us.”

“You know I will.” He hopped into his big rig and pulled the thing forward.

Ben watched it drive away while his mind went in a million directions. God had no doubt sent him help. He could only hope that the help would keep coming. He’d need all that he could get to find Chasey and Brighton and get them to safety.

He recalled the scripture from Psalm 121 on the dash of Rolf’s big rig.

I will lift up mine eyes unto the hills, from whence cometh my help. My help cometh from the Lord, which made heaven and earth.

The mountains, purple in the morning dawn, rose beyond the city in the distance.

What do I do, Lord?

His answer came in a new calmness that settled and refocused his mind, reminding him that what he should do was rely on his training and his experience. He headed back to Holly House and his cell rang. He snatched it up.

"Chasey?"

"No. This is Calvin. We're going to need you to bring her in. The feds want her now. Her uncle is going to contact her and when he does, we'll be ready. So bring her in, Bradley. We'll guard her with only the most trusted of our agents. We can pick you up. I'm sending a helicopter. It's en route now."

"Send it for me. But I'm alone."

"...Excuse me?"

"Everyone wants Chasey, including and especially her uncle. But no more than I do. Sir, she slipped through my hands."

"What do you mean?"

Now he understood how Rolf felt trying to explain what had happened. "She left my protection, left on her own."

Hurt and misery and anger kept him company, kept him warm on this cold dreadful morning. He ended the call with his chief because there was nothing more to be said. Ben hadn't kept Chasey's brother safe, so Chasey was no longer going to rely on his protection.

He'd failed.

There was no going back.

But he could go forward. He would set things right. No matter what it took or how long it took.

I'm coming for you, Theo Dawson.

Chasey sat in the cab as she was driven across the city. She'd told the cabbie to simply drive, that she would tell him when to stop.

She'd needed to get far away from the scene. Far from Ben. She couldn't look him in the eyes—not when she had been the one to demand they head to Holly House to get Brighton. She couldn't bear to even see the place, because all she could see was her brother being whisked away before her eyes and loaded onto that helicopter with her uncle.

Fisting her hands, she squeezed tight enough that her nails bit into her palms. She couldn't cry, couldn't lose it in front of the cabbie. He might take her to the hospital or simply drop her off on the street, not wanting to deal with an emotionally unstable person. But sorrow and frustration filled her to the brim—for herself, for Brighton and for Ben. She couldn't imagine how Ben must be feeling at this moment. Surely by now he knew that she had fled his protection.

She shoved aside that grief before it could overwhelm her. Right now she had to focus on getting Brighton back, and getting him away from her uncle.

The cab had taken the freeway and merged in with the light Sunday-morning traffic. Better than Monday-morning rush-hour traffic. The thought made her suddenly remember her job. If she wasn't back at work on Monday, her boss would wonder where she was. He might think that the stalker she'd alluded to had finally caught up with her and called the police.

Wait a minute. She was never going back.

I'm never going back. I don't even have a home. Again, she held back the tears. She had to concentrate on getting herself somewhere safe.

"Can you turn at the next exit?"

The cabbie steered the vehicle off the freeway onto a frontage road where several hotels and restaurants were slowly coming to life in the early morning. "Just stop at the gas station up to your right."

It'll be better if he doesn't know exactly where I go, in case he's questioned later. Anyway, I can walk from there.

He did as she asked, pulling into the gas station parking and stopped. She paid him with her credit card, thankful that she still had her emergency pouch with her from when she'd gone running…how many days ago was it now? The pouch also had some cash, but she chose to hold on to that. There didn't seem to be much point anymore in disguising her location by avoiding credit cards. Her uncle had seen her at Holly House. Someone had found her at her house and followed her almost the entire way here. Hiding had accomplished nothing. Uncle Theo knew where she was.

Chasey watched the cab drive away and immediately missed the warmth from inside the vehicle. Pulling her coat tighter, she waited until the cabbie was out of sight, then kept walking down the sidewalk along the street perpendicular to the freeway.

Chasey wasn't sure what she would do, but getting somewhere warm and safe for the moment seemed like a good idea. Of course, she'd been in the cab of Rolf's semi and that had been warm and safe. But after her uncle had abducted Brighton, she'd known it was time to go it alone. He was in control now; he held everything that mattered to her, and she didn't need Ben or anyone else standing in her way and preventing her from getting to Brighton.

And her uncle would reach out to her soon. She knew it in her bones.

She was surprised Uncle Theo hadn't closed

in on her where she'd stood on the lawn outside Holly House and grabbed her, too. But even if he'd let her go in the moment, she expected that he would be reaching out to her soon. He would use Brighton to reel her in. And she would go willingly.

The easiest way for him to contact her would be via her cell phone. Though Ben had taken out the battery and SIM card, she'd kept them on her. It would be easy enough to slot them back in. Attempting to turn on her phone wouldn't do any good unless she charged the battery—it had died while she'd been calling Ben from the marina after that terrifying attack at her home. But it only took a minute to duck into a drugstore and buy a charger cord. As soon as she got somewhere where she could plug it in, she'd be back in business.

She frowned as she considered that others would be able to find her, too. While she actually wanted to hear from her uncle, in the hope that it would lead to a reunion with her brother, Chasey wasn't in a hurry for federal agents to find her. They'd never agree to let her meet with her uncle. So she'd have to keep her phone use minimal, and do her best to stay off the radar in other ways. She'd used her credit card, and they could trace the card to the cab, but that was it.

Beyond the more obvious hotels along the freeway, she spotted a smaller motel—new, but not as flashy as the others. At the motel, she used her cash to secure a room.

Finally, she used the key card to open up a room on the second floor and felt that *déjà vu* moment as she walked in. After the incident in the hotel last night, she made sure to note the exit and how many doors down it was in case of another fire—on the off chance that someone started a fire to flush her out again.

But that wouldn't be necessary this time.

She would go willingly to her uncle. To find and save Brighton.

Her uncle wanted her, and the feds probably wanted her, too.

And that was why she had to leave Ben's protection. At some point he would have had no choice except to give her up to his superiors. At the same time, she wasn't sure that he would have. Maybe it would have been better to give him the chance to make that decision. To choose her over what his superiors or the feds wanted him to do. But it wasn't right for her to put him in that position, and on top of that, it was too risky.

Chasey had survived for years working for Theo Dawson, and knew how to be tough in the face of danger. She had faced that danger every day for six months after the murder she had witnessed, until she had finally gone to federal agents and given them what they'd wanted in exchange for protection for her and Brighton.

In the end, Chasey could only ever trust herself, and she would do well to remember that, no matter how much she wanted to trust Ben. He was a good man. A good deputy US marshal-slash-inspector, whatever he called himself.

She put the battery back in her phone and plugged it in, then sat on the edge of the bed and stared out the window as the sun rose over the snowcapped mountains.

"You're a good man, Ben," she whispered to herself. "I know you're trained for this, but it doesn't mean I can let you risk your life for me or ruin your career over me."

And now she was talking to herself.

She slipped the SIM card into her cell phone and turned it on. *Let the games begin.*

Fear gripped her. All the running she and Ben had done had come down to this moment.

She let the tears she'd held back after walking away from Ben freely flow as she poured her heart out to God. He already knew what was inside her heart, but still, she needed to connect with Him.

Lord, all I ever wanted was to live a peace-

ful life. I never asked to be the ward of a criminal, and then to be forced to work for him. Kept in line by fear and intimidation tactics. When will it end?

Her cell buzzed with a text. Chasey stared at the message, unsure if she could believe what she read.

FOURTEEN

At the US Marshals Service regional office in Denver, Ben paced a small room he'd been relegated, staring at his cell phone. Now that he was no longer on the run, he was back to using his regular cell. He tried to contact Chasey, figuring she would be using hers, as well, but the call had gone straight to voice mail.

He wasn't sure if her uncle would continue to try to find her. Dawson had a chance to grab her back there on the Holly House lawn but instead he'd simply waved at her.

Ben was still trying to make sense of it all, to understand why the aggressive search for her had concluded with her uncle's seeming indifference to capturing her. All he could come up with was that they had led Dawson to Brighton, though that still left many unanswered questions. Why all the attacks, if capturing Chasey hadn't actually been the goal? Why would he want Brighton and not Chasey? Was this about revenge for Chasey's testimony, or was there something more at play? Ben scraped a hand through his hair.

He hadn't gotten enough sleep and couldn't be sure of anything at the moment.

Chief Calvin opened the door and walked in. He'd arrived in the Denver field office a few minutes ago. As WITSEC inspectors, their tasks were secretive and the rest of the deputy marshals didn't usually know what they were working on, or whom they were working with. It was the best way to protect their witnesses.

Except in this situation, the system had broken down.

"Bradley, have a seat," Calvin said. "Your pacing is driving me nuts."

Ben turned to look at his chief, meeting Calvin's level gaze. "You can only protect a witness who wants to be protected, Ben. You shouldn't beat yourself up over the fact that she walked away. Participating in the program is always voluntary."

Reluctantly, Ben slid into the chair at the table, facing his chief. "She wouldn't have walked away had things not gone south. If her uncle hadn't gotten his hands on her brother."

And it was all on him. Hurt and pain twisted in his gut. Anger burned through his chest.

Calvin set a bottle of chewable acid relievers on the table and pushed it across to Ben. "I know how you feel. But you can't give up now. She needs you whether she realizes it or not. Now, with Dawson escaping, we're putting together a task force including the FBI, DEA and the USMS. Chasey Cook is still your witness. She stood firm and did her part through the trial, and we promised to protect her. I believe her stepping away is a momentary lapse."

Ben nodded. Though he appreciated his superior's words of support, he knew this galvanizing effort to find Chasey had as much to do with the fact that the feds wanted her uncle back as it did with providing protection. He uncapped the bottle in front of him and grabbed a couple of the calcium tabs. He chewed them up, disliking the powdery taste.

"We're all in this together," Calvin said. "When one of us suffers, we all suffer." He tossed a file on the table.

Ben stared at it for a moment. "What is it?"

"While you've been busy with your witness, we've been digging deep. Secured WITSEC data was accessed by one of our own."

"As we suspected."

"We have systems in place to keep our witnesses as safe and secure as possible. Most of the time they work."

Ben waited patiently. His boss was obviously

building up to something. Ben had a feeling he wouldn't like what he was about to say, but that didn't mean he wanted to wait to hear it. Just... *Get to the point.*

Ben leaned back in the chair and tucked his chin. He tried to hide his attitude, but he couldn't help it.

Calvin slid a photo print out of the file. "Is this the man you saw at the pier?"

Ben stared at the picture. "It was dark. I can't be sure. But it could be him. He's a deputy marshal?"

"No. He was impersonating one of ours that night, after stealing a uniform. The actual deputy was forced to access the database through threats to his family. Once he'd turned the information over, he was taken captive for several days to keep him from having an attack of conscience and revealing what he'd done. The information led to the attacks on Susan and then Sheila before Chasey was found. The deputy was finally released and immediately turned himself in."

Ben pounded the table and bolted from the chair. "He's all right now? His family is safe?"

"Yes."

Ben sighed. "I'm glad they're all right, I'm glad we have answers for how the leak happened, and I'm very glad to hear it wasn't someone willingly selling out witnesses. But answering those questions doesn't change the mess we're in. Chasey's in the wind, and Brighton has been taken. We probably led Dawson to him."

"Intel is telling us that he has known where Brighton was staying this entire time."

"What? How?"

"We learned that Brighton has received a call from his uncle, communicating via his lawyer, once a month for the last year."

"What? And Chasey didn't know? She wasn't informed?"

"Someone on staff was paid to keep it quiet."

Ben fisted his hands and slammed them on the table. "We need to find her! To find them both."

"And we find the brother by finding our witness," Calvin said. "The FBI is following all leads. We have every reason to believe her uncle will contact her. The task force meets in half an hour in the main general conference room. Be there."

His boss left Ben standing there. He stared at his cell and called Chasey again, but got no answer. He left her a voice mail. "This is Ben, Chasey. I—I'm worried about you. Please call me. Please let me help you… I…" Emotion twisted in his throat and he couldn't speak, so he ended the call. He'd almost said, "I love you."

I love you.

He loved her, but that didn't do either of them any good. What an idiot! He had fallen in love with her before, but he couldn't be with her then, and he couldn't be with her now.

Until… Until the threat of reprisal was extinguished. That might never happen.

Ben headed down the hallway to the general conference room. There, he met the representatives from the other agencies joining together to bring down Theo Dawson. But when it was over, he knew nothing more than when he'd walked in. He left the meeting with one imperative.

Finding Chasey.

So nothing had changed for him. It was like the chief had said—everyone wanted her, but Ben didn't appreciate the reasons.

Essentially, she was bait.

If you hear from her, Bradley, we need to know where she is. Contact us immediately. The words from the FBI special agent kicked through his gut. No one wanted to hear from Chasey more than Ben, and his job was to protect her, not use her to draw her criminal uncle out.

They had already gotten a warrant to search for her cell phone so they could try to track her.

But Chasey was smart, and even though she

might have turned her cell on briefly so she could contact her uncle, he would bet she had turned it off now and was on the run again.

Chief Calvin stopped Ben as he exited the conference room and tugged him over to the side and out of earshot. "Her safety is our priority." He leveled his gaze on Ben.

"Understood," Ben added, averting his gaze. He didn't want his boss to see just how emotionally involved he truly was.

The chief got a call and left Ben to stand there and wonder just exactly what the other man meant. Yes, he was part of this team to locate and recapture her uncle, and they wanted to find Chasey as part of finding Dawson. But Ben had his own agenda. He had to put Chasey first—over and above the team's task.

Ben exited the front of the US Marshals Service office building into the cool, crisp day. The sky had cleared to a bright blue. Snow melted into slush along the streets and sidewalks. Outside the building he could hear the traffic had picked up, even for a Sunday. He'd missed church, of course, and would have to listen to his pastor's sermon online later.

He pressed his back against the cold brick of the building and attempted to let his thoughts clear.

Then he prayed.

"Lord, I don't understand why any of this has happened or why Chasey is now out there alone and on her own. I don't understand why I couldn't keep her and her brother safe. And I don't know what You want me to do next. Regardless, please keep Chasey safe. Please help us bring this criminal down without harm to Chasey or her brother."

His cell buzzed, signaling that he'd received a text. He pulled up the message from a number he didn't recognize. His heart pounded as he read the words.

Ben, it's me. I know where he's taking Brighton.

Okay, what do I say next?

She hadn't really thought this through so well. As soon as she had received that text, surprisingly from her brother, she had told Brighton to hang tight and not to worry. That she would come for him.

What she hadn't said was that she would come for him despite the fact that their uncle expected her, even wanted her, to come for Brighton.

She had saved the number from which he'd contacted her, then bought a burner phone at the gas station and turned her own cell phone off. She had fully expected her uncle to try to reach her. And maybe Brighton's text had been part of Theo's plan to lure her.

But she didn't think so.

Brighton was smart as a whip in some areas, although he couldn't communicate or do things on his own very well. Still, if something excited him, he could get his message across.

Private jet landing remote airstrip on island. North side away from hurricane. Uncle afraid of hurricane. Hurry, Kelly.

Chasey had immediately thought of the summer place where their mother had taken them, and that last summer they had shared with her. They had stayed on a remote island in the Caribbean with its old sugar plantation built like a fortress to withstand the hurricanes.

If Uncle Theo had taken Brighton there, then what was his plan? Would he still try to get to her, too?

If her uncle didn't come after her, call her or reach out to her, then she would have to go after Brighton. But to do that—especially now that she had an idea of where he'd been taken—she needed resources. She couldn't do this alone. She couldn't just hitchhike or take a cab to a Caribbean island. Even a commercial flight would be a tricky prospect. As winter and snow season was picking up in the United States, hurricane season in the Caribbean was winding down—but as long as the storms continued, flights to that island were few and far between.

As she sat there wondering what she would do next, her cell rang.

Ben.

Her throat constricted. She didn't want him to persuade her to come in to be protected. But in addition to his help, she wanted to hear his voice.

She answered. "Ben..." His name came out breathy, and tears clogged her throat. "I'm so sorry. Please, I'm so sorry. I had to leave."

"It's okay. Calm down." Just hearing his voice did more for her than she would have expected. Her decision to flee Ben's side had been the right one. But oh, had she missed him. So much that she couldn't resist sending the text, opening up a dialogue, even if it put her at risk of being found by the federal authorities she was sure were looking for her. She hoped she wasn't making a mistake by talking to him now, especially given what she was about to share.

"I need to know if you're safe, Chasey. I'm worried about you." She could hear the concern in his voice, which increased her regret at leaving him behind when he'd worked so hard to protect her.

She hung her head and thought about just how alone she truly was. "I'm good for the moment, but I don't know for how much longer."

"What can you tell me about your brother?"

It was interesting that Ben didn't ask where she was, though his first concern had been for her safety.

"I need to *get* to my brother. I need to get him out of my uncle's clutches. But I can't do it alone. Please don't tell anyone else. I'm concerned that somehow my uncle will find out that I know where he has taken Brighton and then move him again."

Ben hesitated and, for a moment, Chasey wondered if she'd lost the connection. "Ben?"

"I'm here. You're my priority and—" another hesitation, another breath "—Chasey… I'll do my best to help you. I'm sorry that I failed you and that your uncle was able to get to Brighton."

"Please, don't apologize. It's not your fault. If anything, you can blame me for skipping out on you. But because I did, I now know about where Brighton has been taken because he contacted me."

"He told you where he is?"

"Not exactly, but he described enough about

it for me to recognize where our uncle must have taken him. I can't get there on my own. Can you meet me?"

"Yes. Just tell me where you are."

"Promise me you'll come alone. Promise you won't tell your boss where I am."

"You should know the feds are in on the search for your uncle. We're working together. They want me to find you. They've asked me to tell them if you contact me. We know who gave up my witnesses now. Your uncle hired someone to kidnap and threaten a marshal. But the man turned himself in as soon as he was able to. That means the leak in information has been plugged."

Chasey blew out a breath. "You're saying you trust everyone. Is that it?"

"Yes. Still… Because you asked me to, I'll come alone. And I won't tell anyone we're meeting."

"Well, even if you've caught one guy who'll admit to handing over information, I'm not so sure my uncle hasn't influenced someone else to keep tabs on things. I can't afford to trust anyone else, Ben, not with Brighton out there somewhere." She held back the tears threatening to once again choke her.

Her uncle was proving to be more resourceful than they could have imagined—getting his hands on Brighton like that when his location was meant to be so secret and so secure was proof all on its own.

Chasey gave him an address. "Wait for me. I won't be there when you arrive. But I'll come to you."

Because she would have to be sure he wasn't being followed before she revealed herself.

More lives than her own depended on it.

FIFTEEN

Ben wished he had Rolf sitting in the semi just waiting to help. He wished he had *any* backup that he could truly, fully trust to follow his lead and keep all information to themselves. But he couldn't shake the fear that Chasey was right and, even now, Ben shouldn't trust anyone. So even though it went against all of his training, he followed through on her request.

She'd told him to come alone, and Ben wouldn't betray her trust.

Instead of going back inside the US marshals' building, he headed around the corner and down the sidewalk until he came to a busy intersection. He tried to act like he was out for a walk to clear his head. While he walked, he called for an Uber ride. Was he being followed? Watched by the agencies on the task force? Did they suspect he would go behind their backs if he heard from his witness?

Like his boss had said, Chasey was his priority. Ben hadn't needed that from Calvin because, to Ben, Chasey was his priority no matter what his boss—or anyone else—said. Once he connected with her in person, and learned more about what was going on and where Brighton had been taken, he would work to convince her they should call in the feds to take down her uncle and get Brighton back.

After Ben had gone a couple of blocks, he stopped and waited for the silver Ford Focus—his Uber ride—to show up. A minute or so later, he got into the vehicle with a guy named Cam. Ben instructed Cam to drive him across town and had him stop two blocks down from where he was supposed to meet Chasey.

He would walk the rest of the way, pausing in the shadows now and then to make sure he hadn't been followed. He would let Calvin and the others know he had heard from Chasey in his own good time.

Across the street, Ben spotted the Laundromat where he was supposed to meet her. Kind of a strange and unexpected place to meet but that must have been the point. She wasn't there, and he recalled she told him to wait for her there. He figured she had wanted to watch for a few minutes to make sure that he was actually alone and hadn't been followed.

He understood her hesitancy. Suspicion and

wariness had crawled over him, even in the marshals' office in the conference room with several other deputies and agents. He was sure that most of the agents were good, decent people who genuinely wanted to do the right thing. But it only took one person who could be bribed, blackmailed or threatened, and all the information they had could land in the wrong hands.

There was a reason that WITSEC inspectors kept to themselves protecting their witnesses.

"You look kind of lonely." The sound of the familiar voice drew his head up. But he didn't look to his left, where he knew she was hiding in the shadows.

"Yeah." *I'm lonelier than you know.* "I was just waiting to make sure that I'm really alone."

"I think you are." The wariness she'd tried to hide broke through the cracks. "You want to join me?"

"I guess we're not meeting at the Laundromat?" Ben pushed off from the wall and strolled around the corner between the two separate strip malls, stepping into the shadows. At the sight of her safe and sound—though still in danger—relief rushed through him, sending his heart rate jumping. In her hazel eyes, he thought he saw that she was equally ecstatic to see him.

Ecstatic?

Yeah. Thrilled. Relieved. Overjoyed.

"Ben..." She hurried forward but held back. Would she have jumped in his arms if she hadn't stopped herself?

If she had gone even one step farther, Ben would have caught her and pulled her close. He wanted to catch her up against him even now. He held her gaze for a few breaths, taking in her thick red hair and peachy-dream features. When he finally found his voice, he said, "I was so worried."

She nodded. "And I'm sorry."

They could talk about this later. "Let's get somewhere safe. Where are you staying?"

"I've got a room at the Cottage Inn Motel around the corner. We can talk in private there."

He shadowed her around the back of the buildings, through another alley and then to the motel. She unlocked the door and he followed in after her, his mind going in a million directions.

Inside the room, she flipped on the lights.

Ben took a seat at the small corner table. "I'm here like you asked. I didn't tell anyone we talked. No one has followed me—that I know of. Please, Chasey. Tell me what you know."

"I turned on my phone, thinking that my uncle would try to get in touch, but Bright texted me. He struggles to communicate verbally, but he can text a few words. And he told me enough that I know where they're headed."

"And where is that?"

"An island in the Caribbean. We used to vacation there in the summers with Mom. We saw my uncle there, too. We stayed at a big house on the island that used to be part of an old sugar plantation. It's just a vacation house now, but it's built like a fortress."

"Do you know exactly where the island is? I mean there are, like, hundreds of islands in the Caribbean."

"Yes, I remembered the name and then I pulled it up on a computer at an internet café so I could write down the longitude and latitude. It's technically within the United States—part of Puerto Rico's many islands. The name is Isla de la Alegría." She passed the coordinates she'd written down to Ben. "It means Island of Joy."

He stared at the longitude and latitude. "And you're sure this is where your uncle and brother have gone."

"As sure as I can be. I need your help to go there and get Brighton back. Please help me."

He couldn't help the frown that emerged. When he saw her dismayed response, he realized that Chasey had seen his hesitation and misunderstood. He rose and grabbed her hands.

"I'll help you. You know I will. You and Brighton are my priority. But in going there, we need to recapture your uncle and bring him back, otherwise what's to stop him from coming after the two of you again next week or the week after? But if we are going to capture him, it'll be a bigger job than I can handle on my own, especially since we don't know how many men he has with him. Frankly, even going in after Brighton will be difficult if we don't have more backup. I need to tell the task force that's been put together where Theo is so they can bring him in." *God, please let her understand.* "It's the only way we can safely get to Brighton, don't you see?"

"No. What if there's another leak of information? I can't risk losing Brighton again. If the wrong person finds out, Ben… You can't promise me that won't happen."

He nodded and stared at the floor, an idea forming. "Okay. All right. I'll go. I'll go alone and I'll get Brighton out safely. Then I'll inform my superior, who will tell the team about your uncle and where he can be found."

They weren't going to like it.

Chasey nodded, looking relieved. "That plan sounds okay, but you're missing one piece. I have to go with you, Ben. You can't communicate with Brighton like I can. I need to be there for him. We go together."

Ben rubbed his mouth. He hated the idea of her in harm's way. On the other hand, he remembered how difficult it had been to communicate with Brighton when the siblings were in protective custody prior to the trial. There were days when Chasey was the only one who could get through to him. How much harder would the situation be if Brighton was already frightened and upset after his abduction? Chasey really was the best option to get him to leave quietly.

"All right. To do this, to go in there to get Brighton out, we need a good plan," he said. He wasn't sure even a good plan would be enough, but he would agree to her terms for now.

"And that could be a problem. We don't have time to sit around and plan this out. We can talk about it on the way there. We have to hurry..." Her features twisted as she took two steps forward and then she pressed her forehead against Ben's chest and sobbed.

He wanted to wrap her in his arms and hold her forever. Protect her. His heart ached for her and, finally, he gave in, wrapping his arms around her.

He said nothing because what was there to say? Instead he held her until she stopped sobbing. He had a feeling she had been holding back this entire time, and whatever it was she was about to tell him had pushed her over the edge.

He would wait patiently until she was ready.

Chasey sniffled and looked up at him, her eyes and nose red. Her gaze emanated just how vulnerable she was.

"Brighton told me… He's scared."

She wiped a hand across her nose and stepped back. "Look, I know my uncle. I know how he thinks. They might be on that island for now, but I'm sure it's just a stopping place while he waits for his terrorist buddies to pick him up and get him to a new location in another country far away and out of our reach. If we don't get to Brighton now, I know that I will never see him again."

A lump grew in her throat. She was asking so much of this man. A deputy marshal, her handler, inspector, whatever he wanted to call himself. He was all of those things, but he was also so much more than that. He was her friend and one thing she knew about Ben was that he was trustworthy. So she'd ask him these questions just once, and trust that the answers he'd give her would be the truth.

"Well, Ben, what next? You are going to help me, aren't you? If not, tell me now. I don't have time to waste. I need to save my brother." She left out that she didn't exactly have a plan B if Ben decided not to help her, after all. What would she do? Hightail it out of here and rent a private jet to the Caribbean?

She scratched her head. She could actually do that. She had a little bit of money tucked away. A trust fund her mother had left her that her uncle hadn't gotten his hands on. But she'd never wanted to touch it, mostly keeping it for Brighton in case something ever happened to her. Someone had to pay the bills to care for him. Government payments, disability, none of that would cover it all.

I'm all he has...

She turned her back on Ben, not wanting him to see her anguish.

"I already told you I would help." He spoke over her shoulder, his breath tickling her ear.

She hung her head, sucked in a bolstering breath then turned to face him. She could hug him. Jump in his arms. She could even love this guy because he was just so lovable. Those dimples appeared in his cheeks again and her stomach flip-flopped like she was in middle school, crushing all over again.

Be still my heart.

No, seriously. Be still. The "don't fall in love with him again" plan has already fallen through. The best you can hope for now is to stick to the "get used to the idea that you can't be together" plan.

Ben gently lifted the curtains to peer out, an all too familiar sight.

Lord, please just let this be over soon.

He turned to her. "Everyone is looking for you. You know that, right?"

"Everyone?"

"The FBI. The US Marshals Service. Do you want me to keep going?"

"No."

"Probably your uncle, too. He could have been the one to send that text, or coerced Brighton into sending it. You know that, right?"

"Either way, I have to go. He either took Brighton as retaliation, to hurt me, or because he has some other use for him. Even if this is the best-case scenario and he took Brighton because he cares about him and wants to look after him, he's not someone Brighton would be safe around. Nothing about my uncle will ever be safe."

Ben's eyes took her in, and she thought she could read what he was thinking.

You're not safe anywhere near your uncle, either.

He held his hand out to her and she took it. "Let's go get your brother back."

She nodded, wanting to say thank you, but tears choked her throat. Chasey pushed down the emotions and the gratitude. She needed to be strong for what came next.

He eased the door open and peeked out. Once he slipped out the door, he edged over to the alley and she followed close at his heels. The evening was getting on and it would be dark in an hour or so. Chasey thought the shadows worked well for them, just in case anyone had followed Ben.

She crept with Ben through the alley, wishing they had time to make better, more careful plans to get to Brighton. But then again, they could have that discussion on the way.

"I don't know how you planned to get us to the island, Ben, but I have an idea."

Two men suddenly stepped into the alley and faced them. One aimed a weapon. A gunshot rang out as Ben shoved her out of the way behind a dumpster. Chasey screamed and covered her head, waiting for more gunshots as Ben fired back. But gunshots didn't resume. She turned to see Ben lying in the alley, horribly still.

Another man was standing over him, not one of the two who'd been facing them a moment earlier. He'd come from behind them? Ignoring the others, she scrambled over to Ben's side.

"Ben?" she whispered, her heart jackhammering. "Ben!"

The man grabbed her and pulled her away.

"Let me go!"

"You're coming with us."

She felt a prick in her arm and darkness edged her vision. She kept her eyes on Ben, sprawled on the ground in the garbage. Was he dead? *Ben...*

Darkness took her.

SIXTEEN

Head pounding, Ben blinked his eyes open and then shut them fast again when someone shone a flashlight in his face.

"Sir, please open your eyes again," the paramedic instructed. "I need to check for signs of a concussion."

He had just opened his eyes again to comply when he heard his name being called out.

"Bradley!" The shout came from the other end of the alley. Ben sat up and rubbed his head.

He recognized his chief's voice as the man rushed forward, standing there with barely leashed patience as the EMT continued checking him over.

"Definitely a concussion," the paramedic concluded, and then spent the next few minutes going over the dos and don'ts for his recovery before trying to convince him to ride back to the hospital for more advanced screening. Ben refused, thanked the paramedic and turned to the chief, who didn't wait even a second before asking for a report.

"What happened?" Calvin asked once the EMT had gone.

"Chasey." Been looked around. "We were ambushed."

Calvin slowly shook his head, confirming the grim news Ben expected.

"There's been no sign of her since she left you and the trucker outside Holly House," Calvin said. "Unless you have information that's more up to date?"

"She texted me," Ben admitted. "Asked for my help. She said her brother had reached out to her, also via text message, and that she thought she knew where he'd been taken. We were leaving to go after him. Heading out when two men appeared in the alley. They fired at least one gunshot. As I turned to shove her behind the dumpster, another got me from behind."

"So there were three men?"

Ben nodded. "No bullet holes in me, so he must have slammed his gun into my head."

Ben could feel the knot, still throbbing from where the paramedic had poked at it. "They must have just left me here. I'm guessing someone found me?"

Calvin nodded. "A busboy came out of the

restaurant over there to toss some garbage in the dumpster. When he spotted you, he called 9-1-1. Once they found your ID, I got the call and came straight over."

Ben checked his watch and felt his stomach sink. He'd been out for over an hour. Who knew where those men had taken Chasey? "You don't have any leads on where she might have gone?" he asked.

"None at all, but it looks like someone else picked up on at least one clue that we missed, if men took her."

"Her uncle."

"You're sure it was Dawson behind this second abduction in twelve hours?"

"As sure as I can be." His gut clenched. Some deputy marshal he was. He couldn't even protect the girl he—what? Loved.

The chief grabbed his arm as if to steady him, and urged him out of the alley. "Let's get back to the offices before too many others start asking questions."

"The task force doesn't know you found me?"

Chief Calvin shook his head with a grimace. This man had Ben's back. Always.

Because of that, Ben would press his case. "Chief, I'm going after Chasey. I know where they're taking her. We were going together to get Brighton. She asked for my help and I promised to help her. I'll go it alone if I have to. With or without your help. But I would prefer your help."

Calvin sighed. "I thought you might say that." He and Ben stepped out of the alley. "My rental car's across the parking lot."

"Thank you." Ben turned and shook his boss's hand. "For always having my back. I couldn't have done any of it without your help."

"You're welcome. As US marshal WITSEC inspectors, we couldn't work very well and get our jobs done if we didn't have each other's backs." Calvin dipped his chin, his dark gaze boring into Ben. "Now...what do you need from me?"

Ah. Good. The man understood. "Thanks for offering to assist. I need a flight to the Caribbean tonight."

Calvin's eyes widened. "The Caribbean?"

"Yes. I have longitude and latitude coordinates of where Chasey believes Brighton has been taken. It's likely the same place those men are taking her, too. I know the others want to know where she is and will want Dawson back, but I don't think we should call in the cavalry until I have verified that they are there."

"Do you think she had good intel?"

"She seemed absolutely certain. It's a place

she went with her mother long ago—so it makes sense. She said there's a fortified old plantation there."

"I see." Calvin gestured toward his vehicle as he disengaged the locks.

They got in and Calvin started the car along with cranking up the heat.

"It's a sticky situation here. I'm in a hard place, Ben. There's an alphabet soup of agencies that will want to know you've been in contact, and everything your witness has told you. And considering the shape you're in with that concussion, they might have a point when they say that someone else could be the right man for this job."

Ben rubbed his aching head. "I hear what you're saying, but I'm the only person to do this. I'm the only one she trusts. You tell the FBI if they want Dawson, then they are going to have to wait their turn."

Calvin grinned. "I'm glad you're on my team, Bradley."

"Can you buy me some time or not?" Ben asked. "That's all I'm asking. Let me get a few hours ahead before we alert everyone about the island's location."

"We need to be close enough to be able to send the cavalry in when you need more help. I'll get you on that flight out tonight using

USMS resources. In the meantime, I'll inform them we believe Dawson is somewhere in the Caribbean. That will get the forces moving in that direction so they can be on standby."

Ben nodded and ignored the pain in his head. A few ibuprofens would get him through. He hoped.

"One more thing, Ben. Something you might not have considered that could be a problem for you."

"Oh yeah?" He wasn't a bit surprised there was more.

"A hurricane is bearing down on the Caribbean even as we speak."

The rolling motion, followed by the sudden jerk to the right, broke through the thick fog of Chasey's drugged state and brought her fully awake. Wariness, resulting from years of learning to be cautious, prevented her from jerking wide awake, from crying out or gasping for breath…or even opening her eyes.

Breathe in slowly. Out slowly. Even and steady.

Do not move.

Chasey felt the memories flood her mind even as she tried to get her bearings—with her eyes closed. By the motion, the movement—the *turbulence*—she knew she was on a jet. And with that, she knew where she was being taken.

Chasey was being transported to Isla de la Alegría.

Voices spoke in low tones from the seating closer to the cockpit. Maybe if she cracked her lids a bit, she could look around and know more. But she decided she would wait and listen and gather as much intelligence as she could while they thought she was asleep.

One man spoke a Slavic-sounding language. She feared that her uncle was waiting to transport them all to one of several countries where he had offices—the Ukraine, Finland or Lithuania. When he'd first hired her on as his assistant, she'd thought that working for her uncle would require her to learn one or all of the languages from the countries in which he was involved, but he had actually forbidden it. She had no doubt that was to keep her less knowledgeable of his operations. But that, of course, hadn't been enough to keep her from gathering evidence against him and turning him over to the authorities. Knowing her uncle's ways, his methods of retaliation when he felt betrayed, she knew to expect certain death.

Oddly, knowing that she was indeed on a plane headed back to him and to Brighton gave her a measure of comfort.

This was where she'd wanted to go, even if she'd hoped to arrive secretly and with Ben by her side. She had to save her brother, and if she couldn't save him, she had to be with him to make sure he was all right. And if he wasn't all right, she had to be with him to comfort him. They would suffer together instead of alone—and for as long as she had, she'd keep working to find a way to set Brighton free.

Her thoughts jumped to Ben. She had been counting on him to help her save Brighton.

Tears welled behind her lids. Was he even still alive?

Boisterous laughter coming from the men up front startled her out of her thoughts. It also reminded her to refocus her efforts to listen to their conversation to try to extract a few key words. They were speaking completely in their own language, but she heard the word *hurricane*.

Just the word made her heart sink.

If there was even any remote chance that Ben was alive and that he would come for her and Brighton, the hurricane would likely prevent his rescue attempts. She blinked her eyes open and stared out the rain-streaked window. More turbulence shook the plane, and she could feel the fuselage vibrating all the way to her bones.

Were these guys out of their minds to be flying in this weather?

One of the men she recognized from the alley glanced back at her and realized that she was awake. He didn't grin or sneer or laugh. Instead he spoke in hushed tones to his partner in crime. Had they been instructed not to harm Theo Dawson's niece? It was possible. After all, she hadn't been handcuffed and she couldn't feel any bruises to indicate that they'd been rough with her while she was unconscious.

But why take so much care with her now? What about the previous attempts to snatch her? The man in her house had seemed bent on hurting her, if not killing her. Or so she had thought. But he wasn't there. These men were, and they seemed to have been instructed to leave her alone.

She gripped the handrests as the plane descended for a rough, stressful landing. Clenching her teeth, she squeezed tighter, as if her efforts could somehow save her. But her attempts to hide from her uncle had gotten her nowhere. She hadn't been able to protect Brighton, either. It was becoming increasingly clear to her that she had no control over her life at all.

Chasey closed her eyes and tried to hold back the tears. But despite her best efforts, a few tears slipped passed her lids and down her cheeks as she prayed.

When I am weak, Lord, You are strong. Please be strong for me and Brighton, Lord. Show us a way out of this and please send us some help. And, Lord, I pray that Ben is still alive and that he's okay.

The jet landed on a small airstrip. Opening her eyes, she noted a couple of hangars off in the distance. They were heading in that direction. No airport terminal waited for her to enter and collect her nonexistent luggage at baggage claim. The rain slowed, though, as the jet taxied closer to the hangar. Through the window she glanced at the gray sky and noticed the bands of clouds. The hurricane hadn't even truly started yet. It was still making its approach.

At least she could take comfort in the fact that her uncle would probably not try to flee the island to another country—say, Lithuania—until the hurricane winds died down.

The plane taxied right into the hangar. Next to an old blue SUV, she spotted two figures. Her uncle stood watching, and next to him…

Brighton.

The tears broke loose then. "Brighton," she said aloud, although she knew he couldn't hear her—probably couldn't even see her from this angle. Just saying his name made her smile.

A man suddenly took the seat next to her and tilted his head closer. He spoke in low tones, with a thick accent that made it hard to understand as he held up plastic ties. "If you don't cooperate."

She felt his eyes on her, waiting for her acknowledgment.

She stared at the zip ties then looked up at the intimidating foreigner. "Please don't bind my wrists. I promise to cooperate."

"Good. If you don't, your brother gets hurt."

The cruelty of those words accosted her. She wanted to spit in his face. But she didn't dare act out. She couldn't risk any retaliation against her brother.

And on top of that, she had to admit that she was scared for herself. It seemed all too likely that—given her uncles' anger with her—the trip to this island had been a one-way trip for Chasey.

SEVENTEEN

Legs shaking, Chasey stepped out of the private Learjet and took the short steps to the ground. From where he stood next to the SUV, her uncle's face projected a weird combination of a smile and a sneer. It was as if he was trying to smile for appearance's sake, but struggled to contain his anger for all the trouble she'd caused him.

Brighton's expression, however, was the complete opposite. Her brother stared at her, unsmiling, which told her he was stressed. What was he thinking or feeling? Was he scared? She hoped he wasn't, but she couldn't imagine him feeling comfortable with this much uncertainty. He preferred a rigid environment to feel safe and secure.

Neither of them had anything like safety or security here on this island in the middle of a storm with Uncle Theo. She wanted to cry, but even she wasn't sure what she'd be crying for.

Fear? Frustration? Relief at seeing Brighton? Anxiety over what the future held for them?

Chasey chose to focus on the joy of being with her brother for the first time in a year. Ignoring the two henchmen who had remained at her side to keep her in line, she rushed forward and grabbed Brighton, hugging him to her.

Even though she knew he didn't generally enjoy being touched, he would often let her hug him and hold him because he knew how much it meant to her. And, at times, being held brought him comfort and soothed him when he was distressed. She couldn't think of a more stressful situation than this.

Brighton wrapped his arms around her—which told her that he must have really missed her, as well. She held on to him as if for dear life, and let the tears surge.

"I've missed you so much!" She eased away from her brother.

He'd always had the brightest joy-filled eyes—to go with his name. She was glad that the brightness hadn't diminished, even during their abductions.

"Let's go," her uncle said. "We need to get to shelter before the storm hits full-on."

The place where they had stayed as kids with their mother was built like a fortress and had already weathered many hurricanes. The fact that it was still standing proved that they had nothing to fear there—nothing except for her uncle.

Now that she was here on Isla de la Alegría, her memory flashed with her mother's smile and laugh. She'd been so happy. The place had belonged to a friend.

A friend. Had that been her uncle? Had it belonged to him? If so, then the feds could easily find it, so she doubted it was in his name.

She climbed into the back of the Cadillac SUV, right next to Brighton, who sat in the middle. Her uncle sat on the far side of the bench seat, while two henchmen sat up front. The two on the plane with her had taken another vehicle, while another man—the one who had taken Ben out—stayed behind in the hangar.

Chasey reached for Brighton's hand and squeezed, but he pulled away.

Okay, so that touch had gone too far for him. Message received. She'd respect her brother's boundaries, but still wished she could have the comfort of a hand to hold. *Oh, Lord, how are we going to get out of this?*

She stared out the window at the familiar mountainous island covered with a luscious rainforest and palm trees. Rain cascaded down the window, filling her with a sense of hopelessness. But she couldn't let it bring her down.

Brighton was depending on her.

The SUV pulled into the circular driveway in front of the massive three-story plantation house. They exited the vehicle, rushed up the cobblestone walkway and steps and then through the double doors into the foyer.

She looked up at the spacious house. It looked different to her now than it had when she'd been a child. The biggest different, of course, was that she couldn't hear her mother's laughter. Still, Chasey doubted that even if she heard that now, it would extinguish the fear that pulsed inside her.

"Brighton," Uncle Theo said, "you understand your sister and I need to catch up?"

Brighton's big eyes widened. He pulled out his iPad and typed in "Okay" and the iPad spoke for him. He pressed a few more buttons and the device spoke again. "Going to my room."

For all practical purposes, Brighton could communicate—but the activities of daily living, managing financials, knowing how and where to get and make food, and even feeding himself, often failed him. But that was not to say that he wasn't intelligent. On the contrary, many extraordinarily difficult things came to him with utter ease. He could even be considered a savant when it came to computers. It was with machines, in truth, that he was most comfortable. Social situations tended to make him uneasy.

He turned and left her standing there with the two henchmen and her uncle. *Wow, thanks, Brighton.* But even if she felt a little abandoned, the truth was that she didn't want him present for whatever awaited her next.

Brighton slowly moved up the massive staircase without looking back at her.

"In my office." Her uncle's tone commanded.

A henchman grabbed her arm and ushered her through a doorway down the hall. She took a quick look around, mentally rolling her eyes at the lavish carpets and furnishings. The house's remaining decor made her uncle look like some aristocrat out of place and time.

He nodded to the man, effectively dismissing him, and settled in the chair behind his ornate desk.

"Have a seat."

Chasey did as she was asked, relieved to have a chance to hide the way her knees shook. She needed to remain calm and strong, and give away as little as possible—all while hoping for someone to make a mistake or slip up in some way that she could take advantage of so she could escape with Brighton.

He stared at her, trying to browbeat her with a mere look.

"What are you going to do with me?" She purposefully left Brighton out of it.

He toyed with a pen on his desk. "I haven't decided yet."

"You sent someone after me. I was under the impression..." Should she really speak the words and remind him that he'd wanted to kill her?

"I would never send someone to do a job that I wanted to do myself."

"So, you sent someone after me to capture me and bring me to you so you could kill me at your leisure if you chose to—but you are still deciding if you want to kill me or not."

"Yes. I'm too frustrated right now to talk without losing my head." He got up and walked around the desk.

He wrapped his hands around her neck and started squeezing. What an idiot she'd been to simply sit there and let him approach. But she hadn't expected him to actually do it.

Not here. Not now.

The pressure started building in her head and she tried to pull away from him but his grip was like iron.

The door opened and Uncle Theo dropped his hands. He smirked at her. "I wasn't actually going to kill you yet."

Wrapping her own hand around the tender flesh of her neck, she gasped for breath. *You could have fooled me!*

"What is it?" The way he snapped at the newcomer showed his displeasure. "Never enter my office without knocking."

"Someone is landing at the airstrip."

"What? Who could possibly…?"

Uncle Theo slowly lowered his gaze to her. "Put her away."

Put her away? Like she was an unattended toy or a dish that needed to be moved to the sink? She was manhandled out of his office and down a hallway, not upstairs with Brighton. Wouldn't they be allowed to be together? She didn't like this. Not at all.

"Where's Brighton?" she asked the henchman. "I want to be with him. Take me to his room?"

"We have a special place for you," the man said. "Your uncle doesn't trust you."

"But I've cooperated. Doesn't that get me any privileges—like time with my brother? Please."

The brute continued to escort her down the steps into a basement.

More like a dungeon.

"You should be comfortable in this room. You have a bed, chairs, a desk. Paper and a pen." He opened the door and thrust her forward.

She stumbled into the spacious room. To her surprise, Uncle Theo hadn't thrown her into an obvious dungeon, after all. The room actually seemed rather comfortable. Except… "There are no windows. Plus, there's hurricane coming. What if it floods?"

He shut the door and locked it from the outside. She heard a bolt, too.

Chasey wasn't going anywhere until someone let her out. She curled up on the bed and considered the fact that someone was trying to land. Someone her uncle hadn't been expecting.

Someone who had ruffled his feathers.

Oh, God, please let it be Ben. Please let it be someone to rescue us.

Ben was the only person she'd told about the island. If he had died in that alley, then their chances of escape had died with him. But someone was here. Did that mean Ben was okay? Well enough to come himself—or at least to send someone else?

The sound of the door being unlocked drew her up to a sitting position. What now? The door opened and in stepped her brother.

He held out the iPad, which spoke for him. "I have a plan."

* * *

Ben darted away from the helicopter, the rotors still going. Two more men followed him, splitting up and running for the bushes. Coming to the airstrip was a risk since they had every reason to believe that Dawson was keeping it monitored and would know immediately about their arrival. On the other hand, the airstrip was the only safe place to land, given the wind and the airborne debris. The hurricane was moving in and the ocean waves were growing. He was risking his life and the lives of two additional men by bringing them here. But Chief Calvin had only provided the transportation as long as Ben had agreed to take two additional agents for backup.

Once they confirmed that Dawson was on the island, Ben would notify Calvin, who would then coordinate with the task force to send in a full strike team to free Chasey and her brother. And to recapture Dawson.

His small three-man team had donned tactical gear to protect themselves against an assault—weather or criminals. While the rain wasn't pleasant to be out in, it still felt good to have his feet on solid ground again. The turbulence along the way had mimicked a series of miserably long roller-coaster rides. They'd first taken a jet to Florida and then a military helicopter, capable of handling the winds, had brought them the rest of the way. It hadn't been a stealth approach, but at least they'd arrived safely.

Now to get on top of the hard part.

The entire east side of Isla de la Alegría—Island of Joy—was privately owned by a corporation strongly believed to be a shell company linked to Dawson. A large home—more like a compound, according to satellite images, and almost certainly the plantation house that Chasey had mentioned—was located about three miles from the airstrip.

He and his team members would communicate via their radios, though he imagined that he would struggle to hear anything in this weather. They planned to split up and search the grounds for signs that Dawson was physically there. They'd then meet at a designated location to check in and plan next steps as soon as their tasks were complete. Ben would head straight for the main structure, believing that Chasey and Brighton were likely being held there.

After making sure guards weren't standing around waiting to shoot them near the airstrip, he took off on his three-mile jog in the rain and wind. He kept his breathing steady as he watched his surroundings. Brighton and Chasey were counting on him.

He couldn't let them down this time—his last chance to save them.

He could only hope that he wasn't already too late. Ben wouldn't put it past the man to disappear his niece and nephew.

Spotting the house that looked more like a well-fortified compound, Ben ducked behind a palm tree that swayed in the wind. The weather was brutal—but as long as he wasn't washed away in a storm surge, he would endure.

Besides, an approaching hurricane was probably an advantage. He doubted too many men would bother standing guard at the house in this downpour. And anyone watching through windows or security cameras would have trouble spotting him.

Ben moved from tree to tree, closing in on the structure.

Closer to the house was where he was most likely to find trouble. But he didn't care. He pictured Chasey's face when he'd found her again at that Laundromat.

The way his heart had pounded at the sight of her. How relieved he'd been. Her safety was all that mattered to him. Brighton's safety, too—

because he was an innocent who didn't deserve this, and because he meant so much to Chasey.

Ben took a step out from behind the tree just as an SUV sped by on the road, heading for the house. He dropped to the ground, hoping to stay out of sight. The rain pounded so hard, he couldn't hear his heart, but he could feel the pulse in his throat, the beating in his chest.

His breath caught when he heard the screech of tires, signaling that the vehicle was backing up. He rolled to his back and chambered a round in his firearm. Then he crawled, army-style, through the island grass. With the way the wind whipped around, it was sure to hide any trail he left. From behind a palm, Ben spotted a man in tactical gear, holding a semiautomatic rifle, searching the woods. Looked like Dawson had his goons armed to the hilt.

If Ben could take the man out, then he could also take his vehicle and maybe even his uniform. He just had to do it without alerting to his presence. He preferred to enter the house and find Chasey without setting off alarms. Or, at least, setting off as few as he could. This could be his best chance to get inside.

He crept up behind the man and hit him in the head with the butt of his gun—hard enough to stun him but not to kill him, just as another man had done to him in the alley a handful of hours ago. Ben took the guy's hat, gun and boots.

Now he looked like the bad guys. He didn't know how far that would get him, but he would do his best to use it to his advantage.

Dawson's man trussed and loaded in the back of the SUV, Ben steered toward the house. He parked behind two other SUVs. Uncertainty accosted him. How many men would he find inside? Was he making a mistake gaining access this way? He might be walking into a trap—but staying put wouldn't guarantee his safety, either. For better or for worse, he needed to move forward. He hopped out of the SUV and started around the house.

As a deputy US marshal and inspector, Ben had never found himself party to a covert military operation, let alone as a mercenary. But he imagined the tension and adrenaline he felt now was one that any special forces operative would understand.

A radio squawked—not the one he'd brought for his team, but one from the guy whose place and gear he'd taken. He couldn't understand the question, and doubted anyone could understand him in the storm, but the voice sounded thickly accented.

"Checking the perimeter!" he shouted in reply, allowing the wind to glance off the radio, as well.

He jogged around the house, his weapon at the ready, looking for an entry point. A kitchen maybe. But everything appeared to be locked down tight.

A gust of wind shoved him and he flattened against the wall.

A door opened and a guy dressed like him waved him inside. He pushed from the wall as the rain pelted down. Keeping his head low, he jogged forward. Once inside, the force of the wind slammed the door behind them both. Ben shook the water out of his face.

"Thanks, buddy."

The man's eyes narrowed. "Who are you?"

Ben belted him in the face with the butt of his gun and quickly knocked him out. After trussing this henchman, as well—gagging him and binding his hands and feet—Ben dragged the man down the hall until he found an empty room. He stuck him inside then removed the man's weapons and communication equipment. He left the guard and hurried down the hallway, leaving a trail of water behind him. Wary now of the noise it could make, Ben turned his radio down.

One of his three radios squawked, the voice coming in loud and clear inside the house. Ben jogged back to the entrance he'd used minutes before and, through sheer force of will, opened it, letting the wind howl through to mask his voice as he replied on the radio again.

"Checking the perimeter!" He went with that because it had worked the first time.

Now, time to ignore the radios and find Chasey and her brother. He spotted a set of stairs that led to a lower level. A basement. A lab where they conducted experiments? He shuddered at the thought. Or a dungeon? A prison? Where would Dawson keep the niece who had betrayed him?

Ben crept down the stairwell and found the lower level dimly lit and empty. His hopes sank. If he could have grabbed Chasey and her brother down here, with no one else around to spot them, they could have escaped out the back and taken the SUV.

Wanting to check out the last room, he crept along the wall, wary of what might be hiding behind the shadowed corners. As soon as he stepped across the threshold of the final room, he heard a swoosh. His skin tingled and he instinctively ducked—but not quite fast enough. Pain ignited in his back and pushed him forward. He rolled and aimed his weapon.

She stood over him with a bat.

Recognition flooded him and he lowered his weapon.

"Chasey, it's me!"

EIGHTEEN

Chasey had lifted the bat, prepared to drive it down into the head of what she took for another one of her uncle's guards, hoping to knock him unconscious. Then she would grab his guns and radios and get out of there. She'd already started forward with the bat and couldn't stop her momentum even as recognition hit. Fortunately, Ben rolled out of the way.

The bat hit the floor as she gasped. "Ben!"

She'd feared he was dead. It seemed impossibly wonderful that he was alive and here, that he'd come for her. She dropped to her knees, noticing his face twisted in pain. Chasey grabbed his shoulders. "I hurt you. I'm so sorry. I thought you were—" She looked him up and down. "You kind of look like the guys guarding us."

"That's because I've taken a couple of them out and put on some of their gear." He gripped her shoulders. “Are you okay? And Brighton. Have you seen him? Is he okay?”

Brighton stepped out of the shadows and Ben’s eyes widened at the sight of him. “We’re fine,” Chasey assured Ben. “But we want to stay that way and need to get out of here.”

Ben smiled and hugged her to him. “I’m glad I found you.”

In her ear he whispered, “I was so worried, Chasey. So worried.”

“I’m okay. I can hardly believe you’re here.” She eased back to look him in the eyes. “I was so afraid they had killed you back in that alley in Denver. But you’re here. I can’t believe it. You came for us, and in the middle of this horrible storm.”

“It’s going to be okay.” He released her and scrambled to his feet.

“Your uncle. Is he here?”

She nodded.

Ben spoke into a radio. “Send in the troops. I found them. And Dawson is here.”

The troops?

Ben offered his hand to assist her. “Let’s get you out of here. You and Brighton.”

She got to her feet without taking his hand. “Wait, where are you taking us? Do you know where you’re going? Brighton has a plan.”

Ben blinked. Her reaction exactly, but she

was quick to speak up in her brother's defense. "He's a genius in his own way. A savant. He's been watching everything ever since he got here, paying attention when others are clueless to what he knows. What he can do."

"And that…puts him in danger."

She nodded. "Yes. My uncle never seemed interested in his abilities before, so it never occurred to me. But Brighton told me that's why my uncle wants him—I still don't know for what purpose, yet, but I'm beginning to see the bigger picture here. My uncle seems to need Brighton's gift. But he worried that Brighton would refuse to cooperate. So my uncle brought me here to use against Brighton. He's using us against each other." That wasn't to say that he meant to keep her alive. Maybe he'd still planned to kill her once Brighton finished whatever task he wanted of him.

Chasey could see the confusion on Ben's face.

"We can talk about all that later."

She pulled Ben over to the other side of the large room. "Brighton has his plans written and drawn out so there's no confusion. I'll show you."

She tugged him over to the drawing table next to the wall. Ben stared down at the papers and noticed that they detailed the entire layout of the compound, the cameras, security system fail-safe and guard placements. Then there was a broader drawing of the island. Brighton had marked a location of a boat. His plan included escaping the house and getting to the boat. Chasey hadn't had the heart to tell him they would not be leaving via boat during a hurricane. But if they could escape the compound and hide near the boathouse, waiting to make it out at the first chance they got once the weather cleared, this could work. Her uncle had greatly underestimated Brighton, and it would come back to bite him.

"We couldn't escape without his help. Even with you being here—unless the troops you speak of are already on the island—we can't get past the guards or alarms or cameras without all of this." Chasey looked at Ben. "How did you even get inside?"

"I came through the back door." Ben explained landing in the helicopter then making his way to the house while the two other men hung back and waited for his direction.

A sudden gust of wind buffeted the window and driving rain continued to pound it, underscoring how hard it must have been for Ben's helicopter to get here.

"They know someone landed, so they are onto the fact that someone is here now. That could mess up our plans to escape," she said, but then she took Ben's hand. "Still, I'm glad you're here, Ben."

"I'm not so sure you needed me. Looks like Brighton has it all figured out." He clapped Brighton on the back then recoiled when Brighton frowned. "Sorry, I'll keep my hands to myself. I just wanted to congratulate you. You've done a great job here, buddy."

"We have to turn off the alarms and get past the security team," she said. "But now chances are the alarms won't matter. Sooner or later, they're going to realize they're missing team members and that someone has breached their security. They're going to be looking for us."

Brighton held up his iPad. "The storm," it said. Then he shook his head.

Chasey glanced from Brighton to Ben then back. "You mean the intensity of the storm?" She glanced at Ben. "I don't think he knew about the hurricane or anticipated the intensity of the storm when he made these plans." She snatched up the papers then folded them. "But it doesn't matter. I'd rather take my chances out there than stick around here. There's a village on the other side. We could hide there until we can secure the boat and get out of here."

"We might not even need to get the boat. We just have to wait for help to come," Ben said.

"The troops you mentioned?"

"Not exactly troops. The feds."

"I understand. They want my uncle back."

Ben squeezed her hand, looking at her earnestly. "I didn't tell them where you are, Chasey. The only one who knew was my boss—he arranged to get me here. Now that I've sent out that message that your uncle's presence here is confirmed, he'll be busy notifying everyone else. But you have to admit we need help getting out of this."

She shrugged. "Yes."

Would things have turned out differently if she had at least agreed to talk to the marshals about where Brighton had been taken? Would they now be safe? Or was there someone still working on the inside? With her uncle's connections, she would believe it.

"Come on." Brighton communicated via his device. "We must leave now."

"I agree."

Ben ushered both Chasey and Brighton to the door. Brighton tugged him back.

"He has to lead the way, Ben," she said. "He knows his way around. He has the plan."

"Okay. Okay. Let me be on point to run protection, then." Ben lifted the semiautomatic rifle to emphasize his part, then went ahead of them into the greater room—or dungeon as she'd come to think of it. It was empty and dusty and smelled of mold, after all.

Ben quickly cleared the space.

Brighton moved up the steps, Ben close behind him with the rifle at the ready.

"Expect them to come down here to check on me, so be careful," she whispered.

The door at the top of the steps to the basement would be the riskiest part. Ben started to push through.

Chasey pulled him back again. "Wait. Brighton is allowed to walk around on his own. Let him go first. No one will suspect him if they see him."

Ben frowned and shook his head. She could tell he didn't like this—but it was part of the plan.

The truth was that she didn't like it, either, even though she knew it was the smart choice. She still struggled to let her brother go as he slipped into the hallway.

Ben waited, his ear pressed to the door. A moment later, he reached to open it.

"Not yet," she said.

"What?"

"We wait here for him. He'll be back after he turns off the cameras and security alarms."

A voice resounded in the hallway on the other side of the door. Someone confronting

Brighton? Her heart rate kicked up. He knew his way around. No one should bother him.

"Kelll...yyy." Brighton had used Chasey's real name, and his garbled voice—especially when he was mostly nonverbal—struck terror in her.

That's it—I'm going in now! Ben refused to wait behind the door and do nothing to help Brighton, especially with the sound of the young man struggling, calling his sister's name.

He yanked the door open and stepped out into the hallway, instantly moving to aim the rifle at the culprit.

One of Dawson's hired mercenaries held Brighton by his collar, bullying him.

"Hold it right there!" Ben rushed forward and pointed the gun at the man. "Back away from him."

The man thrust his radio to his mouth to speak.

Brighton punched him in the nose. Ben grabbed the radio from the henchman and forced him down the steps into the basement. Using the tape and ties he'd brought, he bound yet another goon. Just how many men did Dawson have—and how many more would they run into as they tried to escape?

Lord, please let help come for us in spite of the storm.

The rain and wind bashed even this fortress, which only confirmed his feeling that they were on their own for the next many hours. No one in their right mind would travel in this weather.

Brighton and Chasey had followed him back down.

“We’re wasting time,” she said. “If you have to stop and tie up every man you come across, we’ll never get out of here.”

Ben pulled her and Brighton out of the room and to the steps before he spoke. He didn’t want the man he’d just taken down overhearing and then repeating their plans. “I think we should forget about the alarms and security systems. They don’t matter anymore.”

Brighton’s eyes widened. He typed furiously into his iPad and it spoke for him. “Security cameras everywhere. Outside. At marina. On boat I want to take.”

Ben blew out a breath. He doubted they would even get that far in this storm. But how did he convince Brighton?

Chasey touched his arm. “Please, Brighton has a plan. Let’s trust him.”

Even after what had just happened in the hallway? Supposedly, Brighton was allowed to roam the place. Who knew what other rules and expectations had changed?

"We're running out of time to get out of here," Ben said. "Are you sure your plan is still in play?"

Brighton lifted his chin. Ben saw in his eyes that he was sure. Ben also saw how important this was to both Chasey and Brighton.

"We're doing this Brighton's way, Ben." Chasey's words left no room for argument.

If their minds were made up, all he could do was try to protect them. "Let's go then. We're running out of time."

They crept up the steps and Ben prayed they wouldn't run into more of the henchmen. In the hallway, he followed Chasey and her brother. Brighton picked up his pace, moving faster than Ben had seen from him before, obviously understanding the urgency.

If they didn't get out of there in the next few minutes, they would be in trouble.

Escaping in a storm like this on an island was dangerous all on its own. And if they did get out in the next few minutes, they had maybe an hour to find shelter before it was dark.

Brighton opened a door and they followed him down another passageway.

Then he slowed and led them into a closet. What was going on? Ben wondered as he joined them inside. Brighton used a radio that Ben hadn't realized he'd had and began texting a code into it.

Morse code?

Suddenly the door at the end of the hall opened and two sets of boots ran down the hallway.

Chasey whispered, "It's your turn, Ben. There should be one man left in that room."

"What was the plan if I hadn't showed up?"

She lifted her bat. "It would be on me to take him out."

"Wait here."

Ben crept out of the closet and over to the door and banged on it. He kept his head down and hoped that he wouldn't be recognized as the man who'd gained access.

The door opened and Ben thrust his fist into the man's face. He fell back. He was down but not out. Ben aimed his weapon and forced the man to ease his hands away from his gun.

Chasey and Brighton rushed into the room. While Ben zipped plastic ties around the guy's wrists and ankles and tape over his mouth, Brighton got busy at the computer consoles, shutting down the cameras.

Ben glanced at the screens and noticed the hurricane was on top of them in full force. Just what did they think they were going to do outside this structure?

The storm surge alone could bury a good portion of the island, and that wasn't even taking into account the possible damage from the wind or the rain.

The henchman tied up and no longer dangerous, Ben peered over Brighton's shoulder. His fingers flew over the keys, shutting the cameras down. Alarms, too. But all it would take would be for someone to walk into this room and turn everything back on.

One last camera remained on. Chasey pointed to the screen. The boat wasn't on the water but inside a building. Their escape plan was to wait out the storm and, as soon as possible, to get that boat on the water and away from the island. Ben sent a text communication via his radio to the two men who'd come to the island with him. He glanced at Brighton and Chasey, wondering again if they could pull off this plan.

The agents responded that they had been instructed to take shelter and wait for the feds to arrive, or to assist Ben if needed. He relayed the plan about the boathouse, giving the location and asking the men to meet him there, if possible.

The only problem?

It was on the other side of the island.

Brighton stood and Ben thought they were leaving, but the kid moved over to another computer and thrust in a small USB drive.

Ben peered at Chasey and tilted his head in a silent question.

"He's planting a virus. It'll destroy the servers so they can't control anything from here. Once it's all shut down, they will not be able to reboot."

"Why didn't he just do that to begin with?" Ben asked. "Why shut everything down individually first?"

"Brighton has to do things his way and in a certain order."

Ben nodded that he understood. They dashed out of the security room, and Ben cleared every hallway as they moved until they reached the back door.

"It should open without setting off any alarms now," Chasey said.

Brighton wrapped his iPad up and placed it under his rain jacket.

"You ready?" Ben looked at each of them. They both nodded. "I parked an SUV around the side. Let's hope it's still there. Either way, I'll try to get us wheels that we can take to the other side of the island."

Once they opened the door, the wind pressed

in, sending the rain lashing at them. Brighton helped Ben pull Chasey forward against the force. Then they had to get the door shut again. If they left it open, someone was sure to find their egress. He pulled on the door. Brighton and Chasey helped him yank it closed.

This was nuts. He knew it, and they knew it, and the men he would meet at the boat knew it. But their other choices weren't choices at all. Keeping close to the plantation house, they crept to the corner. He peered around and, sure enough, the SUV he'd left remained parked there. The guy was probably still stuck in the back. Ben would like to dump the man, to ensure he wouldn't make any problems for them, but he couldn't justify leaving him in the storm to die.

They ran for the SUV.

"There's a henchman in the back," Ben explained. "Don't bother him."

Ben started the ignition and pressed the gas pedal. The tires spun in the soaked ground and the vehicle struggled to gain traction.

Brighton's device spoke. "Nobody in the back."

"Are you sure?"

Brighton nodded.

Ben decided not to worry about it. They had

a vehicle now. They were out of the fortress. Now they just had to get to safety.

A vehicle appeared in front of them, heading right for them.

"Uh-oh, Ben. What are we going to do?"

"There's only one road out of here. We have to keep going."

Spider cracks instantly appeared as a bullet slammed the windshield.

NINETEEN

Chasey screamed as she ducked. The vehicle swerved off the road but Ben kept steering forward. She held on for dear life. "Brighton, are you hit? Are you hurt?"

She twisted in the seat to peer behind her and found her brother sitting up in his seat.

"Brighton, lie down. You have to duck."

She unbuckled.

"What are you doing?" Ben asked.

"I'm crawling back there with him."

"You have to stay down."

"I have to help him." Brighton was supersmart in some ways and in others clueless.

She climbed into the back as bullets continued to pelt the vehicle—though they came from behind now, since Ben had swerved around the other vehicle.

She settled near Brighton on the back seat. "It's going to be okay."

Her uncle wanted—needed—Brighton for

his exceptional abilities, and he would stop at nothing to find him.

Uncle Theo had to know that Brighton was on the run by now. What measures would he take to capture them again?

As the wind buffeted the vehicle, Ben continued to steer them along the bumpy road, straight into the driving rain. Maybe the troops were on their way to arrest her uncle and get them safely off the island, but it would be hours before they could arrive—even if they attempted to come during the storm. The three of them were on their own—and the thought was terrifying. Next to Brighton now, Chasey wanted to hold him, and decided to risk reaching out to him again. She scooted over into the middle and grabbed his hand.

"You did a good job, Brighton," she said. "We made it out. You shut down their computers, and they won't be able to find us." At least, she hoped they wouldn't. There were only a few roads and she wasn't sure how many men her uncle had at his disposal to help with the search.

"Do you think help will arrive in time to save us, Ben? Do you think they can get here in this storm?"

"I don't know." He raised his voice over the

noise of the storm that filled the cab from outside. "Just pray they do."

"I will. But even if they don't, I trust you to protect us." If there was one thing she had learned, it was that the men in her life needed her encouragement.

The men in her life.

She shook her head and pressed her mouth against the top of Brighton's head. "I'm sorry I went away for so long. I thought it would keep you safe."

He pulled away from her and twisted to face her, then pointed at his chest. "I…keep *you* safe."

She held back her surprise that he'd spoken. The words were sweet. She gave his hand a gentle squeeze, and he allowed it.

Up front, Ben continued driving, fighting to keep control as the wind tried to push them off the road. In the rearview mirror, she could see that his features were tight and drawn as he concentrated.

Behind them, the vehicle they'd encountered earlier was gaining on them.

She leaned forward. "We're being followed, and I don't want us to lead them to the boat. It's the only boat big enough to take us as far as we need to go."

"That can't be true. The villagers need supplies. There must be other boats. Planes, too."

"No..." Brighton suddenly spoke up, sounding agitated. "We go to boat. Boat, boat, boat. We go to boat."

Uh-oh. He was getting upset. Before he'd gone totally nonverbal, he had often gotten stuck on repeating the same words or phrases over and over.

"We will go to the boat, Brighton. Do not worry. But we need to shake the men who are following us. We don't want them to know the boat is special."

Come to think of it, *was* there something special about this boat? Why did Brighton insist this was their only way?

Ben slowed the vehicle to a stop.

Chasey glanced over her shoulder at the headlights still approaching. "What are you doing?"

"There's a fork in the road."

"The left will take us to the village," Chasey told him.

"No. The boat." Brighton started pounding the back of the front passenger seat.

"I have an idea," Ben said gently, clearly trying to calm her brother down. "Be patient, Brighton. I have a plan."

"No. My plan. My plan. My plan."

"Your plan is still in place, Brighton, but we need to take a detour first." Ben turned left, toward the village.

But Brighton opened the door and jumped out.

Ben jammed his foot on the brake pedal as Chasey screamed.

As soon as they'd stopped, she jumped out of the SUV to chase after her brother. Ben pulled off the road, wanting the vehicle well hidden before he headed off after them. He drove through the grass until he could pull the vehicle into the rainforest underbrush. The way the wind whipped and rain poured, the men following from the compound would be hard-pressed to see any tracks. By hiding the vehicle, he risked losing sight of Brighton and Chasey, but if he left the SUV in plain sight, their pursuers would know that they were on foot and would have an easier time tracking them down.

The vehicle hidden, he leaped out, slammed the door and took off in the direction where he'd last seen Chasey.

"Chasey!" He called her name as loudly as he could, but even as he did, he doubted she heard his shout over the storm.

Lord, help me!

Finally, blessedly, he caught sight of her red

hair whipping behind her as she ran. She was going fast, but she still hadn't caught up to her brother. Ben hadn't realized Brighton could be so energetic, or that he could be so adamant about his plan. Why did he think it was so important for them to go immediately to the boat? The question clawed at the back of Ben's mind as he dodged tree branches, the occasional wooden plank and sand carried on the wind.

He glanced over his shoulder, looking to see if they were being followed—thankful when he saw no one behind him. Maybe they had returned to the shelter of the compound to wait out the storm.

But when he looked forward again, Chasey was no longer in sight. "Chasey!"

"Ben!" Chasey dashed from the woods to his left and sprinted up to him.

He held her at arm's length. "Where is he?"

She shook her head as tears joined the rain lashing her face. "I don't know. I don't know. Please help me. I can't lose him now. I've come too far to lose him."

He gripped her arms, fearing she might take off again. "Okay, I'll help you look. But once we find him, we have to get to shelter. We can't stay out in this."

Ben pulled her to him and out of the way as

a large tree branch whipped passed, emphasizing his words.

"What if we don't find him in time? Brighton doesn't understand how dangerous it is out here. He doesn't know what he's doing."

"We'll find him," he said, wishing he felt more confident that his words were true. "Let's go."

He tugged her away from the woods.

"What are you doing? He went that way."

"We're heading in that direction, too, but being in the trees like that could be dangerous."

He cupped his hands around his mouth and shouted, "Brighton!"

Next to him, Chasey did the same.

"If we keep heading in this direction, we'll end up at the boat, right?" He glanced at her.

She shielded her eyes as she stared up at him and nodded.

"We can't leave in the boat until the storm is over. Why is he so adamant about going there?"

"I don't know. He insists he has a plan. Right now, all that matters is getting back together, somewhere sheltered. We can just head to the boat, too, and hope we all make it without getting hurt or running into the wrong people."

And that was the problem with this plan. The wrong people could already be there waiting.

TWENTY

Chasey had never spent this much time out in a hurricane before. She doubted many people had. So she couldn't have imagined how much the battering wind and rain would drain her energy. As a runner, she'd built up her endurance, but now she felt as if her body was failing her. A mile. Two miles. Two and a half, and she thought she might fall flat on her face.

Brighton.

He needed her help. Or so she kept telling herself. She couldn't believe that her brother had actually left her behind in his stubborn determination to make it to that stupid boat.

Pressing her hands over her face, she attempted to shield it from the torturous driving rain and let a few tears fall as she stopped next to Ben. Finally, she dropped her hands as they stood on a rocky outcropping that overlooked the ocean. The wind was to their back, blowing them forward. Eventually, they would get a reprieve as the eye of the storm passed over. But that would be hours from now.

Hours and hours of this.

Ben drew her attention and pointed below them.

A figured, carefully pushing against the wind, was headed for a secure structure out over the water.

The boathouse.

Brighton.

"But, Ben, look." Chasey pointed to a vehicle winding down the road, also heading toward the structure. It wasn't the same one that had followed them. This vehicle was grander. In fact, she recognized it as the one that had picked her up from the airstrip. "I think… I think that's my uncle."

"Along with another of his henchmen." Ben turned to her. "The two agents who came with me were supposed to meet us there. Maybe they are already inside. I need to warn them. Stay here. I don't want you to get hurt. I'll get Brighton. Please wait for me here."

"What?"

"Arguing with me is wasting time. Let me go after him and get him out of there before your uncle gets him."

She bit her lip. "What if he doesn't listen to

you? I mean, he didn't even listen to me when he jumped out of the car."

"He's about to be put into a very bad situation. I think he'll listen."

She swallowed hard. "Okay. Go. Just...go."

Ben frowned. "Look, there's a boulder here. You can duck next to it. That will shield you a little until I can get back. I don't want to leave you here, but I'll come for you as soon as I can."

"It's okay. Go. Get him. I'll be fine."

She watched him climb down the rocks, sliding about halfway down until he was on the road.

She crouched against the rocks, waiting and watching to see if the men she cared about most would come back to her.

Ben hurried across the way and disappeared into the building.

All she could do was pray as she watched and waited. She found a position on the far side of the big boulder, like he'd suggested, and held on to the hope that this would be over soon.

A sound caught her attention. Had she heard gunfire? Gunshots? Chasey stood.

Should she go down to check on Ben and Brighton?

Her brother dashed from the building and rushed along the water's edge, headed for a rising rocky cliff. Ben didn't emerge from the building. What had happened to him? Panic swept through her. It wasn't supposed to happen like this.

She wanted to go to both Ben and Brighton—make sure they were okay—but she had to choose. She was afraid for Ben, but he was an experienced law officer and she had to trust that he could take care of himself. Brighton, on the other hand, needed her.

Heart pounding, she rushed across the road after her brother. Where was Brighton going? He seemed to be moving toward a ridge. The waves crashed against the rocks much too close. A rise in tide would leave him trapped.

"Brighton!" she continued to call as she crawled over slippery rocks.

"Kel… Kellllley!"

She whipped around. Brighton waved for her to join him in a sea cave she'd passed. She climbed up, and he caught her arm and hauled her the rest of the way into the cave. Inside, the noise of the waves and storm echoed against the walls, but she instantly felt the relief from the wind.

"What are you doing here?" she asked. "What happened?"

"Uncle."

"Did he shoot at you?"

He shook his head.

"Ben?"

Brighton stared at her. *Now* he clammed up?

"Where's your iPad?" She looked at his form and realized he didn't have it tucked away in his soaking-wet jacket. He'd probably left it back in the vehicle when he'd run.

"Brighton, you're doing great. You were talking before. Please tell me what happened."

"He's..."

Fear corded around her neck—it felt like it was choking her. "He's what, Brighton? Please tell me."

"Gone. Ben is g-gone."

Sea spray splashed inside the cave, the roar of it startling her. She looked around and confirmed her fears. The tide was rising—either that or the storm surge was moving in. She had a feeling this cave would be under water soon.

"We have to get out of here."

"Going somewhere?" The sound of her uncle's voice slithered up her back. She closed her eyes.

"Look out!" Brighton yanked her forward.

Her uncle lunged for her. Anger spilled from his gaze, and she knew he had finally decided what he would do with her.

He would kill her.

Ben had scrambled up to the cave, feeling battered from his spill into the water, but thankful to still be alive. He'd managed to take out two of Dawson's men, but the man himself had, in the chaos, gotten the better of Ben, firing off a shot that had knocked him off balance and into the water.

Fortunately, there hadn't been any damage beyond getting soaked—and maybe a bruise. The gear he was wearing had protected him from the bullet. He was just glad that Dawson hadn't noticed that, or he might have hung around to make sure Ben was dead. As it was, Ben had managed to get himself out of the water and had seen Dawson heading for this cave. Figuring that he'd find the others there, too, Ben had followed.

When he reached the mouth of the cave, he climbed in, taking advantage of the roar of the storm and the ocean bouncing off the walls to mask the sound of his approach. He crept in close and found Dawson—clearly furious, maybe even murderous—backing both Chasey and Brighton into a corner. Brighton's gaze found Ben. His eyes widened, which had the unfortunate effect of telegraphing to Dawson that someone was behind him.

Dawson whirled around to face Ben. He expected to see the gun from before, but Dawson must have lost it at some point because he only saw a knife.

A growl erupted as Dawson rushed forward, the sharp edge of his knife leading the way. Ben dodged him and jumped out of path, bracing himself to fight not just for his life but for Chasey's and Brighton's lives, too.

Water reached his ankles as the surge quickly rose.

"Chasey!" Ben tried to shout over the noise. "Get Brighton out of here before it's too late."

He landed a punch on Dawson's nose and it exploded with blood. The man once again swiped at Ben with his knife. This time, Ben disarmed him, but the man twisted his legs with Ben's and they both fell. Ben's face was in the water and Dawson was on top. Ben might be the better fighter, but Dawson was heavier—and all he had to do to win this was to keep Ben pinned down until he drowned.

But then, the next moment, bewilderingly, Ben suddenly found he was free. He rolled out of the water, coughing and choking.

Brighton stood over Dawson. "I'll give it to you. Let him live. Let us go."

Ben glanced at Chasey, the same confusion Ben felt obvious on her face.

"What are you talking about Brighton?" she asked.

"Never mind her, boy," Dawson said. "Give it to me. Now."

"Fine," Brighton replied. "Hurry." Without more clarification, he sloshed through the water.

Ben caught up to him, wanting to demand an explanation, but when he got to the mouth of the cave, he saw something that made him freeze in shock.

A boat, out on this crazy water. The coast guard!

He stepped forward and waved both arms. He saw a signal flash in return, showing that they'd spotted him. He turned back to Dawson, Chasey and Brighton.

Dawson had scrambled forward and had spotted the coast guard vessel, as well. With a muttered curse, he stepped closer to Chasey, brandishing another knife, and spewing a stream of threats, trying to force Brighton to turn over whatever it was that he had before the cavalry arrived and took him back into federal custody.

With a quick look at Brighton, Ben rushed Dawson, relieved when Brighton did his part and grabbed one of his uncle's arms. Ben was able to secure the other and disarm the man.

Dawson was still fighting them with everything he had, but Chasey, not about to be outdone, stepped up and popped her uncle right in the nose, hard enough that they could all hear the crack.

With Dawson stunned still for a moment by pain and surprise, Ben was finally able to pull both arms behind his back and use the plastic zip ties on his wrists, the same as he'd done with the others.

"Bradley!" he heard someone yelling from the shoreline. "Bradley, are you there?"

Stepping out onto the ledge of the cave, Ben spotted the two agents who had come to the island with him.

"In here!" he yelled, waving his arm to get their attention. "I've got something for you."

The men were more than happy to take Dawson into custody. Once they had him, and Ben was certain that the threat was over, he turned his attention on Chasey. He wanted nothing more than to pull her into his arms, but she was holding on to Brighton—and he was letting her, which meant this moment was one he didn't feel he could interrupt.

"I think I figured it out," Chasey said, startling him. "I think I know what Uncle Theo wanted from Brighton. It's something he hid on the boat." She glanced at her brother.

He pressed a finger against his temple. "It's in here first."

"What it is?" After what Chasey had told

him earlier, Ben wondered if maybe it had to do with Brighton's computer skills.

"Bitcoin. He has the information on a USB drive and he hid that on the boat," Chasey said.

Ah. Ben nodded. Now he thought he'd figured it out. Theo Dawson had hidden a substantial amount of his money through the use of cryptocurrency, which required many passwords. Without those passwords, no one could get at the money. He wasn't after Brighton's computer skills. He was after Brighton's memory. Theo'd been hiding all the information in Brighton's head so the feds couldn't find and seize it. But he'd needed to get Brighton back to pay for his big escape and his new life.

Ben had to admit, it was brilliant on Dawson's part. Maybe he would have pulled it all off if the hurricane hadn't prevented him from leaving before Ben could get here and thwart his plans.

Once the coast guard vessel had arrived with the cavalry, everyone returned to the plantation structure where the FBI special agents guarded Dawson and his men until they could all safely be transported to the mainland.

Ben found Chasey wrapped in a blanket and staring out the window as she watched the storm. He sat next to her in the window nook.

"You mind if I join you?"

She smiled, but he wasn't sure it reached her eyes. "Please."

He sat extra close to her, glad to feel her warmth, hoping that she appreciated his, too.

"Until this storm has passed," she said, "I won't feel like any of it is truly over."

He took her hand in his and she didn't resist. He watched the rain bash the window and in the corner of his eye, saw her lift her gaze to study him.

"I haven't thanked you yet," she said. "You came here for us, in spite of all of the danger. You kept on fighting and you saved us."

"I don't know that I can take the credit. Seems like Brighton was the man with the plan."

She turned to him, pulling her hand away. "Brighton couldn't have done anything if you hadn't been here with us."

She placed her palms against his cheeks, surprising him. Tears welled in her eyes. "What next, Ben? Where do I go from here? Where do *we* go from here?"

The "we" she was asking about could have been her and Brighton, but he sensed that her question had to do with her and *him,* and these feelings between them that wouldn't go away.

He wrapped his hands around hers. "I think

it's time for some honesty. For me to be honest with myself and with you."

"Honesty is always good." Light shivered in her hazel eyes.

Okay, here it goes. Ben was taking a big risk here. But Chasey was so worth it.

"I love my job, I love saving and protecting people," he said. "But there's nothing I've regretted more than walking away from you last year. I made the wrong choice, Chasey. Um, Kelly."

"What are you saying?"

"I'm saying that I... I love you."

Without another word, he took her in his arms and kissed her thoroughly. Chasey responded eagerly, driving away the last of his fear and regret. When he released her, she was breathless.

"Well?" he asked.

"You want me to be honest?"

"Always."

Tears welled in her beautiful eyes. "I love you, too. I don't think I ever stopped, but I knew you were married to your job. That's always going to stand in the way, isn't it, Ben?"

"Not anymore. I want to be married to *you*. Will you marry me?"

Her face twisted in confusion. "Yes, Ben. Oh yes. But...how can we make it work?"

He smiled. "I'll find a position with local law enforcement wherever you end up. I want to make this work. So what do you say?"

"I wouldn't go back into WITSEC?"

"It's your choice. I could go in with you, or you could become Kelly Bradley and trust in the protection of a big law enforcement family instead of the protection of a new identity. I don't think you have to worry about your uncle anymore. Now that the Bitcoin secret is out of the bag, the feds will be able to lock down the last of his assets and he won't have the means to hire henchmen anymore."

Brighton suddenly appeared in front of them. "Say yes… Kelly. We…we can be family. Ben, too."

"Of course." Brighton was definitely included in this decision and family. Ben hugged Chasey and Brighton to him. "I love my family so much," Ben said.

* * * * *

If you enjoyed this story in
Elizabeth Goddard's
Mount Shasta Secrets miniseries,
be sure to pick up these previous titles:

Deadly Evidence
Covert Cover-Up
Taken in the Night

Available now from
Love Inspired Suspense!

Dear Reader,

Thank you so much for reading *High Stakes Escape*! I hope you enjoyed the story as much as I enjoyed writing it. Stories that take the characters on the run are certainly fun adventures to write and usually take me to places I hadn't planned. For example, I hadn't planned for Rolf to show up and, to me, he's like that person that God places in your life to encourage you at just the right time. He's the perfect example that even in the most extreme circumstances, God is always there with us. Sometimes we don't have to look any further than the people in our lives.

On that topic… I definitely planned for Chasey's brother, Brighton, to make an appearance. His character is an amazing and unique person partially originating from my own amazing and unique child. There are no words to describe how precious my son is to me and how dearly I love him. I thank God for him every day.

I pray that you can see and feel God working in your life and that you especially appreciate and pray for the people with whom He has surrounded you.

I love to hear from my readers. If you'd like

to find out more about my books or to learn ways to connect with me, please visit my web site at ElizabethGoddard.com.

Many Blessings,
Elizabeth

Get 4 FREE REWARDS!
We'll send you 2 FREE Books
plus 2 FREE Mystery Gifts.
LOVE INSPIRED SUSPENSE
INSPIRATIONAL ROMANCE
Evidence of Innocence
SHIRLEE McCOY
LARGER PRINT
LOVE INSPIRED SUSPENSE
INSPIRATIONAL ROMANCE
Alaskan Rescue
TERRI REED
ALASKA K-9 UNIT
LARGER PRINT
Love Inspired Suspense books showcase how courage and optimism unite in stories of faith and love in the face of danger.
FREE
Value Over
$20
YES! Please send me 2 FREE Love Inspired Suspense novels and my 2 FREE mystery gifts (gifts are worth about $10 retail). After receiving them, if I don't wish to receive any more books, I can return the shipping statement marked "cancel." If I don't cancel, I will receive 6 brand-new novels every month and be billed just $5.24 each for the regular-print edition or $5.99 each for the larger-print edition in the U.S., or $5.74 each for the regular-print edition or $6.24 each for the larger-print edition in Canada. That's a savings of at least 13% off the cover price. It's quite a bargain! Shipping and handling is just 50¢ per book in the U.S. and $1.25 per book in Canada.* I understand that accepting the 2 free books and gifts places me under no obligation to buy anything. I can always return a shipment and cancel at any time. The free books and gifts are mine to keep no matter what I decide.
Choose one: ☐ Love Inspired Suspense Regular-Print (153/353 IDN GNWN)
☐ Love Inspired Suspense Larger-Print (107/307 IDN GNWN)
Name (please print)
Address
Apt. #
City
State/Province
Zip/Postal Code
Email: Please check this box ☐ if you would like to receive newsletters and promotional emails from Harlequin Enterprises ULC and its affiliates. You can unsubscribe anytime.
Mail to the Harlequin Reader Service:
IN U.S.A.: P.O. Box 1341, Buffalo, NY 14240-8531
IN CANADA: P.O. Box 603, Fort Erie, Ontario L2A 5X3
Want to try 2 free books from another series? Call 1-800-873-8635 or visit www.ReaderService.com.
*Terms and prices subject to change without notice. Prices do not include sales taxes, which will be charged (if applicable) based on your state or country of residence. Canadian residents will be charged applicable taxes. Offer not valid in Quebec. This offer is limited to one order per household. Books received may not be as shown. Not valid for current subscribers to Love Inspired Suspense books. All orders subject to approval. Credit or debit balances in a customer's account(s) may be offset by any other outstanding balance owed by or to the customer. Please allow 4 to 6 weeks for delivery. Offer available while quantities last.
Your Privacy—Your information is being collected by Harlequin Enterprises ULC, operating as Harlequin Reader Service. For a complete summary of the information we collect, how we use this information and to whom it is disclosed, please visit our privacy notice located at corporate.harlequin.com/privacy-notice. From time to time we may also exchange your personal information with reputable third parties. If you wish to opt out of this sharing of your personal information, please visit readerservice.com/consumerschoice or call 1-800-873-8635. Notice to California Residents—Under California law, you have specific rights to control and access your data. For more information on these rights and how to exercise them, visit corporate.harlequin.com/california-privacy.
LIS21R2